ANNIHILATION

NEON
BOOK FOUR

ALLYSON LINDT

ACELETTE PRESS

This book is a work of fiction.

While reference might be made to actual historical events or existing locations, the names, characters, places, and incidents are either the product of the author's imagination or are used fictitiously, and any resemblance to actual persons, living or dead, business establishments, events, or locales is entirely coincidental.

Manufactured in the United States of America

For my eternal dragon

PROLOGUE
DAHLIA

Magnus had been gone more than a month, and I still missed her so much that there was a giant hole in my heart where she was supposed to be. The biggest time that feeling faded for longer than a few minutes was when I visited the memorial I'd left her in Japan.

Somehow I felt closer to her here. I'd grown up around gods, and I still had no idea if there was an afterlife. If Valkyries ferried the fallen to Valhalla when those warriors passed on, then who ferried the Valkyries?

No one had had an answer for me, not even Kirby. She only remembered her many lives, not what came after death.

But when I stood by this tree, in this place, I

swore I felt Magnus. Like, if I just closed my eyes and pushed hard enough, I might shatter whatever veil was keeping my best friend—my sister—away from me.

She never appeared though. I never found a way to break through and grasp her and yank her back to life.

The closest I got to finding her was calling her phone. It was probably stupid, and her voicemail would be full soon, but it made me feel like she might answer.

As people swarmed around me, I dialed Magnus's number. Her pre-recorded message played like always, and the sound of her voice made tears well up in my eyes.

At the beep, I dragged in a shaky breath. "It's me," I said into the phone. "I don't really have anything new to tell you. We're making a plan. We're checking it twice. We're going to Santa Claus the shit out of TOM once everything is ready. As in, they've been naughty and maybe this is more of a Krampus thing, but I hear he's actually real and I'm not sure if it's wise to take his name in vain, and..."

I sighed. "I hope whatever is in the afterlife is amazing. You deserve it." A knot grew in my throat, and I couldn't grasp my voice, so I hung up.

Fen rested a hand on my back, and the heat of his touch both comforted me and made me miss her more. It wasn't fair that I got love and she got death.

He came with me on most of these visits, but kept his distance while I was doing my mopey, missing-Magnus thing—my words, not his.

"Do you want to stay?" he asked, his voice kind.

I shook my head. "It's not helping today. She's not here." Turning, I slipped my hand into his, and pictured NEON so I could take us home.

A loud alarm sounded, jarring me out of grief and making my heart slam against my ribs. What the—?

A look around told me no one else had heard it, so it was definitely in my head. The warning I'd put on the apartment I used to share with Magnus. The ward I'd put up when I moved that space to another realm, to isolate it. Someone was inside.

No one should be able to do that.

"We need to go. Someone's in the apartment." I tightened my grip on Fen's hand.

He wouldn't need to hear more, not that there was more to tell until we got there. I blinked us to the space, and my hammering heart stopped when we appeared in the living room.

I was looking at the back of her head. Auburn hair falling to her shoulder blades. Bragi was with her? What the fuck? And a man I didn't recognize, with fiery red hair.

Fen's tension was tangible.

"Magnus?" I almost didn't dare speak her name. What if the apparition vanished?

As she turned, and I saw her face, I didn't dare breathe. Was she real? It looked like her. Her eyes were red-rimmed. She'd been crying.

Did dead people cry?

I forced myself to take a breath, and reached out a hand for her. If I could touch her, she was here, wasn't she?

Her actions mirrored my own.

"It's really you." I wanted it to be true. *Needed* it to be her.

"Oh my Gods, you're alive." She grabbed my wrist and pulled me into a hug so tight it hurt. "Holy fuck. I saw you die. I thought... Oh my God." She was sobbing.

And I was doing the same. Hugging her, crying on her shoulder. Soaking her shirt and clinging to her so she couldn't stop being real.

When we broke apart, we were both talking at once, half over each other, half finishing each other's thoughts.

"I saw you die. It was horrible."

"So I killed Vidar."

"I was so sad."

"What was I supposed to do?"

"I was broken, or I would've looked for you sooner," she said.

Broken? I looked between her and the men she was with. "Who's he? Why are you with Bragi?"

"I didn't know where else to go. I saw you both

obliterated…" She looked past me to Fen, and her mouth gaped open. "You're alive too."

"Don't sound so surprised," Fen teased. "I'm not that easy to destroy."

"Does Frey know?" Magnus asked.

What the fuck was going on? I didn't care. This was real. She was here. I was confused as Hel, but I was so happy to see her, and my laugh slipped out without my permission. "Of course he does." Wait. Everything she was saying came together in my head. She'd thought I was dead too. She thought Fen was. She thought she'd killed Vidar…

But I did.

"Why didn't you go to Frey if you thought we were dead?" I asked. "He'd never turn you away." And then this would've been over a month ago. No heartache. No endless nights sobbing.

Magnus stared at her feet. "I was so sad that you were gone. And I felt so guilty… Fen was gone. I thought Frey might kill me for losing you, and I didn't have the strength to fight. Especially not him."

I felt her ache the same way I'd felt my own. Bragi was an empath. How was this hitting him? His expression was a mask with a faint frown.

I squeezed Magnus's fingers. "Frey would never turn you out."

"But Bragi told me…" She glanced at him, and his

frown deepened. "That they'd spoken. That he'd confirmed you were gone..."

What? Bragi spoke to Frey? About us?

Fen's growl reflected the anger building inside me.

"If that conversation had happened, we would've had this reunion ages ago." I stared at Bragi, and Magnus did the same.

I'd spent weeks grieving. Mourning. Feeling like I'd betrayed Magnus for having a life while she didn't.

"You knew." The accusation in her voice was thick.

Bragi gave a brief nod. "I did."

He knew we were alive. She was alive. He was the one being who could've ended this.

I didn't like him before, but now... The hate was real.

"How long?" Magnus asked.

"The day you woke up." Did Bragi feel even the littlest remorse? He had to know how much venom was being directed at him, but he didn't look the least bit bothered. Was he feeding off us? Did this give him some sick thrill? "I did it to protect you," he said. "And I'd do it again."

"What the fuck?" My question came out louder than I intended.

"You did it to keep me." Magnus's voice had slipped into that icy sort of calm that meant more danger than her shouting. "To trick me into loving you."

He did what to her? I was going to kill him. Now? Or wait until she'd said her piece? I squeezed Magnus's hand to let her know I had her back.

"I'll explain if you'll let me." Bragi was calm. Collected.

Infuriating. My dragon wanted to rip his throat out, and next to me, Fen's wolf stalked near the surface, ready to beat me to it.

"I'm listening." The edge in Magnus's voice said she'd already written him off.

Good. I hope he was choking on what we radiated.

"The day you woke up, I got a call from Vidar—"

Fen's growl bolstered me but didn't erase the churning in my gut. Vidar was still alive too? *Daddy fucker.* "Vidar's dead. I saw him die." I didn't want his surviving to be real, but I knew it was. I'd also seen Magnus die, and she was here.

Bragi was focused on Magnus. "Vidar promised me that if I kept you with me, if I kept you away from him, he wouldn't hunt you. You were hurt. You couldn't access your Valkyrie powers— I did it to keep you safe."

"I never asked you for that." Magnus was furious.

"I would surrender so very much, to keep you by my side."

"You barely know me."

"I love you, Magnus."

This was like watching a tennis match. Fen growled, and I tensed. Now we could destroy him, couldn't we?

Magnus shook her head. "Fuck you. You obsessive, fucking fuck. You don't love me; you want to possess me."

"I—"

"Stop." Magnus's shout echoed off the walls. "Don't open your mouth. Don't even think my name. Get the fuck out of my life, and pray I never see you again."

"Mag—"

"Get. The fuck. Out."

I felt a wave of my own magic wash over me, and I knew instantly she'd banished him from the room. From the realm. From our lives. She was wearing the ring I'd left at her memorial. She'd been there and I'd missed her. By hours? By minutes?

It didn't matter. I had my sister back, and she looked heart broken. I pulled her into another hug.

She recovered enough to introduce us to the man with her, Nicodemus—Nico for short. She still seemed friendly with him, so whatever he had to do with Bragi, apparently he wasn't a part of the deception.

It was good someone kind was looking out for her.

He insisted on leaving, to let us catch up, and Fen insisted she was coming back to NEON with us.

Not that I would have allowed otherwise. It was his and Frey's club, but it had become my home, and I wasn't going anywhere without Magnus.

Nico promised to find Magnus and swore to her he didn't know what Bragi was hiding. She seemed to believe him.

Fen, Magnus, and I send Nico on his way.

I wasn't ready to let Magnus out of my sight, so I followed her into her old bedroom to pack a bag so she could come with us. She wanted to get rid of every reminder of Bragi, including what she wore, since he bought it for her. She stripped out of her clothes and tossed them in the tub, and I lit a small, controlled fire with the snap of my fingers, to burn everything for her.

I'd gotten control of my powers when I saw her die. It was like a switch flipped, and I knew who I was. But I would've given up being a dragon in a heartbeat, to have her back. Fortunately, I didn't have to.

I wanted to assure her again she could've called us, but would Frey have killed her if she lived and Fen didn't? *Of course not.* Maybe.

She dressed in her own clothes, and crammed several days' worth of the same into a duffel bag. "Seriously. The only way I could have more toxic taste in men is if I found one who was literally made of toxins."

"There's probably a god of poison out there somewhere." I tried to keep my voice light, but I wasn't sure I managed. "Don't fall for him."

"No? Might be less harmful." Magnus's laugh was weak. "We should find him or her. Hook me up. Why do I keep fucking the wrong gods?"

"You used up all your luck finding me." I grinned, hoping to help her feel a little better.

"I might have."

"This isn't your fault." I meant it. When she tried to argue, I cut her off. "I'm not done talking good about you, bitch. You love completely. You trust without reservation. You have so much heart—"

She shook her head. "No. I'm done with that."

I hoped not. I slung her bag over my shoulder. "Don't let Bragi or Vidar or anyone take away who you really are."

We rejoined Fen in the living room, and the three of us blinked back to NEON.

Frey stared at Magnus with wide eyes, and when he hugged her, she looked like she was going to cry again.

Amid her apologies, I gave him a rundown of what I'd learned so far, and he scowled when I told him how Bragi had kept her from calling him. How and why she'd been locked away from us this whole time.

Frey assured her she was always welcome here, and promised to go grab us food, so we could go upstairs and catch up.

Frey and Fen, and now me, lived in an apartment above the club. When Magus was here, she stayed next door.

As we headed up to her new-old place, Magnus was quiet. This was usually where I'd talk to fill the empty space, but even I didn't know where to start. I knew what had happened, but I wanted details. I wanted every bit of information she'd give me, and I doubted she was in the mood to share at the pace I'd want.

Frey was back within minutes with food. "From the vendors on that street you love in Shanghai."

"Thank you." I gave him a quick kiss and closed him outside in the hallway.

I found Magnus in the kitchen, sitting at the table and staring at her hands. She was here. She was alive.

But she wasn't all right, and I didn't know how to help her.

Keeping her grounded might be a start. And getting some good, old-fashioned take-out from the other side of the world into her.

I laid out the food in paper trays and wrapping, and made sure Magnus was eating before I did the same.

"I swore I felt you." I picked at a steamed bun as I

spoke. So many times, and some days the feeling was so strong..." She'd been there, and I hadn't looked hard enough. "I convinced myself I was imagining it. I'm sorry."

"Same." Magnus shoved piece after piece of meat from a kabob into her mouth.

I wanted to ask which part she was agreeing with, but I suspected it was all of it, and that she wouldn't answer anyway. "It was so strong one day..." I sighed at the memory. Why hadn't I found her? "I dragged Frey and Gwydion into the fae realm. But there was nothing."

Magnus froze, then turned wide eyes toward me. "Fucking asshole." There was venom in her words. "I was there. I swore I felt you. You must've been so close. I was going to hunt them all down." She radiated fury and I felt the same. "For putting Vidar in a position to kill you. For creating TOM to begin with. For... I didn't care. I wanted the board to suffer."

Yup. Felt one hundred percent the same. "He's still out there, and there has to be a reason he hasn't come after us yet." I was so sick of gods and their stupid riddle-logic and their manipulations and their hiding and killing and—

"Every time we try to out-think Vidar, we get fucked." Magnus sank lower in her seat with a sigh. "We don't even know how he made each of us think we'd watched the other die..."

As she trailed off, the answer came to me. *Fuck.*

Never underestimate an enemy, and we'd done exactly that. Pretended she wasn't a threat. Written her off. Moved on to the next threat without eliminating the old one. "Minato," I said at the same time as Magnus.

When we were younger, when we were on campus, TOM trained us and our fellow students to hunt potentials. People who may become gods or other supernatural beings in the various prophecies that the board members of TOM expected to destroy them.

Minato was one of those potentials. She was also the point where Magnus and I decided we were done with TOM. We were going to run far and fast. As part of that decision, we saved Minato. She'd already been dancing at NEON, and Fen and Frey agreed to keep her safe.

She turned on us as repayment.

Her potential was realized when she became a Baku—a being who fed off dreams. She could see them and create them as well. Including waking nightmares. Apparently this was her latest way to torture us on Vidar's behalf. It made the most sense.

"Can you find her?" Magnus asked.

Now I was the one sinking into despair. Supposedly I had the power to feel other magical beings. One of my gifts, courtesy of having Vidar as a father and Skuld as a mother, was that I could sense various energies *out there*. I'd even built a computer program unknowingly that fed off my gift. But, "I couldn't even find you."

"You didn't know you were supposed to be looking, and you almost found me regardless." Magnus's sadness had faded. It wasn't gone, but her excitement for this idea was masking it. "Bragi worked hard to keep you from locating me and you almost did anyway. And you have the program you wrote to help."

He did *what*? If I ever saw him, I'd dismantle him the way I had that steamed bun. But not have him for dinner, because eww... And that analogy had just gone *way* off the rails.

Magnus's idea was giving me hope, and I wanted to focus on that. We would find Minato. We'd start by making sure she never did something like this again, and we'd move on to Vidar.

We discussed other details of a plan, but silence settled in the room again. This was good. This was a direction.

Magnus wasn't moving. She'd gone still and was staring at her hands.

Because she was here, but what she'd gone through the last month... I'd had Fen's support. Frey's. She'd been in a mind-fuck of a world where she thought people cared about her, and Bragi was just—

I mentally snapped off his head with my thumb, and physically moved to her side of the table. I wrapped her in a tight hug from the side. "You're here now."

"I know." She covered my arms with hers and leaned into me. "And it'll be okay." Her voice was raw. "I'm so glad I have you back, and I needed to know Bragi was a piece of shit, so it's not like I lost anything."

But she had, and even though I could be here for her, I couldn't heal her. That was something I'd make every single god involved in this pay for. Painfully.

We spent the rest of the night simply existing in each other's company. Having Magnus here was soothing, and I hoped I was doing the same for her.

The next day, Nico was back. That seemed to lift her spirits slightly, though not by much. When she left with him, I hoped it would help heal more of her turmoil.

But when she called me a few hours later, tormented and with grief gripping her tone, when she told me he was dead...

Would our world ever be right again?

CHAPTER 1
DAHLIA

Look, ma, I'm a stripper.

My dragon-mommy would be so disappointed in me. My father certainly was, or I assume he wouldn't be trying so hard to destroy me. Then again, supposedly they only had me so they could train me as an assassin to kill their enemies, and to see if I ever manifest as anything more powerful in the process.

Joke was on them—I'd become a dragon myself. But even more impressive, I was the headlining dancer at an exclusive burlesque-club-and-safe-haven-for-immortals.

As I shimmied on stage, removing a piece of clothing at a time in an agonizingly slow seduction, *Mr. Crowley* played over the speakers.

NEON had always packed in the clientele, but I drew in even more people. Though I couldn't see beyond the stage lights, into the darkness, I still knew what was there. A club that was the perfect blend of modern and classic, decorated in dark, polished woods and neon lights that only illuminated specific parts of the main room, and let the patrons hide in the many shadows.

And there were a lot of them out there. Some came to see me dance, and others in hopes that they'd witness the train wreck of destruction next time Daddy Vidar—god of destruction, and all-around asshole—sent someone after me.

And just as many were here to feed off my grief. Immortals were twisted fucks, and my show had gotten darker since I thought I'd lost my best friend. The songs had more bite and the dances themselves had picked up a sort of desperation to go with the sensuality. It was easier for me to pour my grief into my performance than lock myself away as I mourned Magnus.

On stage, I tossed aside the final piece of clothing I would remove, leaving me in pasties and frilly panties. Nights like tonight, I was glad I wasn't one of those who could feel emotion, even just the lust that fed Frey, one of the owners of the club.

But I still knew something was out of sync with the world. With NEON. I had Magnus back, but she was missing something. She'd changed. Fen and I had done the whole *I love you* thing with each other, but something kept me apart from the man he'd loved for ages—Frey.

We all three still fucked. No reason to waste good attraction and orgasms, and as a god of sex, Frey certainly didn't mind feeding off the lust I generated on stage, but something wasn't right between him and me.

I finished my set, took a bow, and gathered my discarded clothes before strolling off stage.

The dancing used to be nothing more than a rush of arousal for me. I liked knowing all those eyes were on me, but then only Fen and Frey could touch.

Since I'd gotten better at controlling my dragon powers, the performance also carried with it a sense of power. Of control. I wasn't sure I liked that side of me, but I was certain it was related to my dragon.

As I passed the curtains, a vivid image flashed in my mind, and I faltered. I leaned against a nearby wall for support, and let the too-real colors and sounds and smells roll through my mind.

Sometimes the images were the visions that came with being a dragon—movies of the future that played out in disjointed pieces like a poorly pieced trailer. Other times they were flashbacks. Memories of dreams planted in my head by a vengeful god, and other past traumas.

I'd had to learn to control and accept the dragon visions. I didn't like the flashes of the future, and I refused to acknowledge them as the only path. But if I didn't recognize them and let them happen, they blended with the ways TOM had tortured me, and would have driven me insane.

This one carried a sense of foreboding, but so did a lot of them. Without context, I would store the dragon vision with all the others, in a massive mental archive of *bad things are going to happen because the gods suck.*

"Are you all right?" A kind voice yanked me from my head.

I looked up to see one of the other dancers standing in front of me, watching me with concern. "I'm good." I tried to smile, and it came out as a grimace.

"Boss wants you in his office. Do you need help getting there?" She still looked concerned.

For some reason I couldn't focus on her, though. Whatever was in my head was fucking with me worse than normal. But if Frey sent someone to fetch me, rather than coming down here himself, I didn't want to take anyone back there with me.

I had no idea what his summons meant—frequently sex, but not always—but it was an unusual way for him to make the request. "I'm good. I promise. Thank you."

I swore she vanished as I pulled on a robe. Integrating the dragon vision, letting it happen without letting it freak me out, was taking more out of me than normal. I strolled toward Frey's office, keeping as much of an air of *collected* around me as I could.

The sex had gotten rougher between all three of us since I lost Magnus. Since she came back. Since I got a lot more control over my immortality and the two gods weren't worried about breaking me anymore. It had always been kinky, but now it had an underlying primal feel to it.

Fuck, sometimes that was exactly what it was— Fen chasing me through the forest. Hunting me...

I hoped this was because they wanted sex. I needed the distraction. The release.

When I reached Frey's office the door was open. I found him at his desk and Fen pacing next to it. When I closed the door, I felt the change in the air. It was like a million needles rolling over my skin then pulling away suddenly.

Frey had moved the room to a different plane of existence.

Recognizing his action was just one more thing I could do as a dragon. It was odd being so in touch with those powers.

The way Fen watched me sent shivers over me. He was big, and all muscle, with dirty blond hair and a stance that screamed *Viking king*. Which he'd more or less been once-upon a time. Or at least the godly version of it. His wolf was near the surface, which meant danger or sex. Or both. Right now, it was growling to be set free. Calling to my dragon.

That put me on edge.

"Good show." Frey dragged his gaze over me. His frame was slighter than Fen's, but still all raw, wiry muscle and strength. He managed that balance of beautiful and terrifying at the same time.

My thin robe didn't hide much. I didn't want it to. "Thanks." Every instinct told me that my being summoned wasn't for after-show boning, as nice as that would be. "What's up?"

They exchanged a glance. One of those wordless looks that made me jealous. That reminded me they'd been together for centuries, and I was still just a baby immortal.

Frey focused on me again. "I have an idea about where Minato is. Not an exact location, but closer than we've been before."

Give her to me. I'll devour her soul. I'll ensure she spends an eternity in torment. It will be the finest feast.

I gasped at the unexpected words. What the fuck? That wasn't...

But it was. That was my dragon. And new. I'd never had that before. If I let the leash off my restraint, the creature would sing in harmony with Fen's wolf, and destruction would follow.

"Are you all right?" Fen asked, a growl cutting through his words.

Why did everyone keep asking me that? "I'm fine."

We were close to finding Minato. The bitch who

betrayed me after I opted not to kill her. The creature who manipulated me. Who made me think Magnus was dead and made Magnus think the same of me.

I wasn't big on vengeance, but this woman... We'd saved her life, and in return she spit in our faces again and again.

She'd tried to take my best friend—my sister—from me. And that wouldn't fly. "Let's go get her," I said.

CHAPTER 2
FREYR

Dahlia's reaction didn't surprise me, and was at least half the reason I moved us before I told her the news. The other half was for privacy. If no one knew where we were, they couldn't listen in.

If Dahlia was driven enough to go now, if she decided not to act rationally, she could change our location as easily as I could. I hoped that the fact that I'd done so to start would make her think twice. I studied her, looking for an indicator of how dangerous this was about to get. Her appearance was deceptive. Dark, long hair she wore up when she danced. Pale skin. Eyes that could see into a person's soul.

Since she'd realized she was a dragon, she carried a new air, but it was still impossible to tell by looking at her that she could snap a mind or a body like it was nothing, depending on which of her gifts she embraced.

"We still have to find a precise location, and If we could go now, what would we do?" I asked. "We're not prepared."

"Prepared for what? She knows we're looking for her. Do you want to pause and do a training montage? Play a little music, pretend we'll be better fighters at the end than we are now?" Dahlia's sarcasm was on-point tonight.

Then again, it usually was.

Fen had stopped pacing, and was watching us with his jaw clenched. I'd known him—loved him— long enough to recognize that meant he agreed with her, but he didn't want to disagree with me.

Which happened a lot more these days than I wanted to admit.

"How are you going to fight her?" I asked.

Dahlia flexed her fingers and claws sprang out where her fingernails had been. Her hand became gnarled and large—dragon talons—and iridescent purple and black scales spread halfway up her arm.

Fen's growl was one of impatient appreciation.

This Dahlia was so different from the brave-but-terrified mortal we'd met years ago. But in a lot of ways she was still the same. Loyal, loving, and fierce. Hating to fight unless it meant protecting those she loved.

All those things were the reasons Fen loved her. I

adored her too, though something held me back from that declaration of *love*. I couldn't name my hesitation, but it was there.

Time for me to be the voice of reason. "Every time you've faced Minato, she's drawn you into dreams. She's fed from you while you faced nightmares you thought were real. We don't know how to fight that."

Dahlia's dragon claw vanished, and she sank onto a nearby sofa with a sigh.

"We're working on answers," Fen finally spoke. He'd vocalized his displeasure with having to wait before she got here. He was a hunter. A warrior. He wanted to find the threat and destroy it.

It had taken me a long time, centuries, to accept that he could do those things—hunt and destroy—without losing himself to his wolf, but Fen was in control.

It helped that he'd recently learned he wasn't responsible for the death of Astrid, a dear friend, back in the day.

"We think Artura might have an idea about how to face Minato," I said. No one in my circle of acquaintances or in Fen's had ever dealt with a Baku. No one we'd asked could tell us how to beat someone who could draw their opponents into a waking dream without warning or any indication she'd acted.

"So let's go talk to Artura." Not too long ago,

Dahlia would've rather died than visit her aunt, one of three living dragons including Dahlia. But Artura had been helping her learn to be one with her dragon, and they were starting to get along.

They weren't close, but they were no longer enemies.

Fen handed Dahlia her purse. "It's polite to call first."

She rolled her eyes but pulled out her phone. "She probably already knows we're coming."

The charge in the air changed, and an invisible sensation tugged my limbs, as if threads ran through each toe and fingertip. I was instantly on alert. "Something's wrong at the club." I rejoined the office with NEON in a blink, and all three of us rushed to the main room.

Everyone was slumped over their tables. The dancer on stage lay in a crumpled heap. Even the bartender had crumpled down behind the bar.

Fen sniffed the air. "Not dead."

Dahlia pressed her fingers to the throat of the nearest patron, under their jaw. "Pulse. They're sleeping."

"Minato." I didn't like this. It could be someone else, but she was the only creature of dreams I knew who would do this to us. The disconcerting thing was, I'd hidden NEON from her. She shouldn't be able to find the place, let alone use her magic here.

We needed more information. I cut a straight

path toward the bartender, Rune. One of the people I trusted most in this place besides the two individuals at my back. I knelt next to him and gently shook his shoulder.

He mumbled something I couldn't decipher, and jerked one foot, but didn't wake up.

"I don't like this." Dahlia's voice was calm, but concern and power undercut it.

I glanced over my shoulder at her and Fen. His facial features were more wolf-like than normal, and his teeth bared in a silent growl.

"Look out," Dahlia shouted.

I caught a flash of purple dragon scales as I spun back to Rune. He grabbed my throat before I could react, and lunged, shoving us both into the bar.

Glasses clanked, wobbled, and rained down around us.

Twisting my fingers, I used magic to yank his wrists away from me and bind them behind his back. A trick I'd learned centuries ago for sex, that these days I used as a weapon more often than I cared for.

Fen's growl would make anyone else's blood run cold, but for me there was comfort in knowing he was ready to interfere on my behalf. He grabbed Rune by the collar and hauled him to his feet.

Rune struggled so hard, his shirt ripped, and Fen gripped his arm tightly before he could tear free.

"You." Rune's gaze was clouded and unfocused,

as if he wasn't here, but when he turned toward Dahlia, his eyes narrowed. "You did this. You did this. She wants you, not us. She's torturing him because of *you*."

Dahlia shook her head. "No. Who is? Who are they torturing?"

Rune lunged again, but Fen held him tightly. "You already know. You did this. You killed him."

"*Rune.*" I forced power into my voice; enough to shake the walls and the shattered glass beneath our feet. "*Wake up.*" We hadn't been able to wake Dahlia when she was caught in Minato's dream, but she'd been there a lot longer. Would it matter?

He snarled and struggled against Fen's grip.

I needed a different tactic.

It hit me. Not all gods spoke to base instincts, but I did. It wasn't a power I used these days, I didn't need to, but when I was younger I'd been happy to whisper to people's lust. To draw out their subconscious desires until it was all they could feel.

Could I override whatever deep-seated fear was keeping him locked in this dream?

I approached Rune and he didn't react. His attention was all on Dahlia as he jerked against my restraints and Fen's grip to get to her. I dipped my head near his ear and grasped the threads of power that lay at the core of who I was.

"Whatever you want, it's yours." My voice was satin and seduction. "Whatever you desire, whoever makes your pulse race and your cock hard, you can have."

Rune went slack in Fen's arms.

Mission accomplished.

Rune's head jerked up again, his eyes wider than ever, and he opened his mouth in a silent scream.

Silence became sound, and a bone chilling *NOOOOO* tore from his throat. "I'll kill you. I'll rip you apart with my bare hands. You'll suffer a thousand lifetimes for what you've done." He struggled harder than ever to break free of Fen, and the invisible bonds that held him.

"We have a bigger problem." Dahlia's voice was drowned out by multiple screams and the sounds of chairs scraping against and hitting the floor.

I spun to see that a large number of patrons were mobile, the same glazed-over look in their eyes that Rune had.

But unlike him, several of them could wield powerful magics and weapons.

NEON was supposed to be a safe haven. No fighting. No outside rivalries. There were wards in place.

The same wards that were supposed to keep Minato from ever touching NEON. The same wards that seemed to have failed.

A fireball flew between us, striking the bottles of liquor that lined the back wall.

Rune broke free as a portion of my bar went up in a flash of flame.

Fen was a wolf in a blink, lunging at the god who had thrown the attack, and standing on his chest to pin him down. A berserker flew through the air and grabbed Fen in a full body tackle, tossing them both to the side.

A billion solutions ticked through my head, each discarded in a blink as being too deadly or impractical.

Fuck.

CHAPTER 3
FENRIR

This fight—any fight—was a glorious thing. Better still, now that I'd faced the demons that divided my wolf and human half, I could be both at the same time. I could keep my wolf form, fight, and still think.

I side-stepped a lightning strike, never breaking my stride, and lunged at the immortal who cast it, pinning them down.

The sound of glass shattering and wood splintering crashed around me. The only drawback to this battle—we were destroying the club.

Oh, and we couldn't kill the people we were fighting, because slaughtering a god or other immortal would bring wrath down on us, regardless of the circumstances. And we had to be careful of the people who hadn't woken up yet. I could smell the immortality on some of them, but others were either mortal or masking their power.

Actually, now that I thought about it, this wasn't a fun fight at all.

"We have to move those who haven't woken up yet." Frey dodged a wild-eyed lunge from Pan. The other god stumbled, but recovered quickly.

Gods who didn't deal much with war didn't used to be fighters, but we'd all adapted over time, and rumor had it, Pan had a few dirty tricks up his sleeves. This could be fun.

I drew his attention from Frey, adding the confrontation to the half dozen I was already involved in. *Can we move them into the back room? Can we keep them there?* When I was in this form, I could still communicate, but my voice was more of a magical sound that would carry through the room, rather than being produced by vocal cords.

"I can keep them there. The only issue will be if they wake up like this." Frey settled himself between two sleeping patrons at the miraculously still intact table next to me.

Dahlia was knocked back when a six-foot leprechaun tackled her. She planted a knee in his gut and sent him reeling. "This is a no-win situation. We don't have a choice if you don't want them here."

Creation, I loved her.

Frey nodded in agreement and vanished with two

beings in tow. The placement of people in the room would make it impossible for him to grab everyone at once, without taking the chairs and conscious people too, so this was going to take him a while.

I ducked under one attack, rolled through another, and came up short when Pan stepped into my path.

He stuck out his foot, catching me off-guard and knocking me off-balance, and drove an elbow into my back as I stumbled past.

Well, fuck.

Dahlia grunted when she took an arrow of light to the shoulder. The wound healed quickly, but the pain on her face lingered. "We have to do more than this," she said.

I supposed. Though this was pretty fun.

"What did you have in mind?" Frey joined us again, having finished his relocation program.

"I don't know. A comically large alarm clock? Can you summon one of those?" At least her sense of humor was intact.

A splash of liquor hit me in the face, and before it blinded me temporarily, I saw Pan smirking through his sleep-induced war face. "*Whatever we do, can we start with him?*" I'd love the chance to see what I could do against a fighter like this, but if I had to hold back, I wasn't interested.

"—don't care—not mine—" Pan muttered as he

lunged toward me. I braced myself, but he veered off toward Dahlia.

He grabbed her hair and wrapped it around his fist, yanking hard and tugging her off-balance. She recovered as he vanished and appeared on the other side of the room. I wasn't sure if she or Frey had sent him over there. I didn't suppose it mattered.

While my first instinct was to shield Dahlia and Frey from any combat, it wasn't practical to indulge that ideal. Dahlia was probably best equipped to fight Pan, given her training at TOM. She was highly skilled in hand-to-hand combat, and had been raised with the mantra of *Victory by any means.*

"Dahlia, you keep him busy," I said. *"I'll hold off the others while Frey figures out how to subdue them."*

Pan charged me, and Dahlia intercepted, yanking him into a grapple. He swung wild at her, she ducked, and he tried to sweep her foot from under her.

She grabbed his ankle and tugged them both into a grapple on the ground. "I assume if this were an anime, he'd probably grab my boob to distract me." As she spoke, she rolled aside, but her robe was caught in the process and pulled away.

"He wouldn't do that." Frey looked bothered by the apology. "No self-respecting god would do that."

Really? *That* was what he was going to grumble about?

"Loki would," Dahlia said.

Like the man said, no self-respecting god.

"I don't care if you go. My heart isn't yours," Pan muttered as he shifted his weight and pinned Dahlia to the ground.

Peculiar thing to say in the middle of a fight, but if he was trapped in a nightmare and thought we were part of that... This could be as bad as when I faced off against Dahlia, before she learned to control her dragon.

Except she hadn't wanted to hurt me. She'd fought that impulse every step of the way, and these beings were indifferent to me at best.

I ducked under a table thrown by an elf, and cringed when it slammed into the stage with a loud crash. *"Can you take their passion away? Or at least mute it?"* I asked Frey.

Because passion fed war as much as it did lust, and if these people were trapped in the heated throes of their deepest nightmares, passion may be making their impulses worse.

"That's not the way I work." Frey's exasperation was audible.

Dahlia vanished from the space she stood in and reappeared behind Pan, to plant a foot in the back of his knees, sending him stumbling. She was getting better and that was a good trick. "It makes sense, though. If you can make passion stronger, you know where it exists in someone. What it feels like. You can dial that down instead of turning up, can't you?

When someone cranks a stereo, they also have the option to turn it down."

"Unless the knob only turns things up. I don't—" He sighed and wiggled his fingers as a fireball flew at his face. The projectile vanished before it hit him, likely sent to a place where it would dissipate harmlessly. "I'd need to focus."

"*We'll hold them off.*" I wanted to feel more glee with my assurance.

Minato had managed to make battle dull.

Inexcusable.

Frey twisted his fingers again, binding Pan's hands behind him. Frequently a dangerous trick with someone wielding magic, but so far he'd kept his fighting physical. Would Frey's bonds hold long enough for him to finish?

Dahlia huffed. "You picked the one guy I'm fighting, instead of the half-dozen facing off against Fen?"

"I need you focused on more than one, and this one seems the most deliberate. He's already exercising some control." Frey stood in front of Pan and grasped his face.

Dahlia moved into a stance next to me. It was easy to fall into combat with her. She had an instinct for where I was going, who I was targeting, and she was skilled at picking her targets.

Frey muttered things I only had half the attention for, as Dahlia and I fought. Frey said something to Pan about letting it go. About not holding on.

"Our past creates us, but it doesn't have to be our future." Frey's words carried a kind of wisdom few people—few gods—would ever recognize. He was beauty and experience personified as he closed his eyes and drew on his power.

A flying kick caught me in the shoulder, knocking me off-guard and forcing my attention back to the fight. I wrangled a nymph with my teeth, as gently as I could. Thank fate there weren't any berserkers here tonight.

"What am I— Freyr?" That was Pan. Confused, but sounding conscious. "What in creation happened to your bar?"

When a fireball struck me in the flank, I growled. The wound healed instantly. The smell of burning fur would linger for days. *Frey, take care of the ifrit next.* Before we all burned down. *Pan, help fight or get out of the way.*

"Why is there anything left standing, to fight?" Pan still stood there.

"We don't want to hurt them," Dahlia said. "They're dreaming, the way you were."

And now we were talking. At least Dahlia was still in the battle, and Frey was moving to the next target. Pan standing there doing nothing was more of a hindrance than holding him at bay.

The leprechaun rushed toward us, and I tensed, ready to protect.

Pan stepped aside, stuck out his foot, and sent the other man stumbling, then used the advantage to pull him into a headlock. "You were incredible on stage." His gaze never left Dahlia.

My growl grew louder. "*Back off.*"

"She's yours, I get it puppy." Pan twisted against the struggling leprechaun, slammed his head into a nearby table, and let him sink to the ground, unconscious. "That won't hold. What's going on?"

Frey restrained the ifrit.

Dahlia broke down the situation quickly, while all of us continued to hold back the tide of attacks.

"So you want these people calm. Complacent," Pan said.

"*That's what worked with you.*"

He grinned and knelt next to the leprechaun. "I knew this was going to be an interesting decade." Pain cradled the man's face in his hands. "I can do that, if your sexy priestess of Athena watches my back."

I stepped between Pan and Dahlia, possessiveness pushing me hard toward wanting to take this fight to the next level. If Pan could help, I'd save ripping out his throat until we were done. "*I'll watch your back, and you'll watch your tongue. She's a dragon.*"

"No shit." He didn't look up from what he was doing.

Dahlia was grappling with the same nymph who had charged me moments earlier. "Yeah, yeah. The baby immortal is unique. Are we fighting, people?"

"Is there a comma in there?" Pan's voice was full of humor.

This wasn't fun. Nothing about this deserved joking. Not when we had to hold back from a real battle. *"Do your job."* I was happy to watch his back, as long as he did what we needed, and he kept his hooves off Dahlia.

As the fight wore on, Frey and Pan worked their way through waking people up one-by-one. Each time, Frey promised to explain, and sent them to the same room as the people who still slept.

When we'd taken care of every patron, NEON lay in shambles.

We could rebuild the bar, though it would take time. But it wasn't safe anymore. For more than a century it had been a safe haven and neutral ground.

And now that was shattered.

"I'll go explain the situation to our guests." Defeat hung heavy in Frey's voice. The pain on his face sliced through me deeper than any attack had.

This club was literally a part of him, and he was my heart. With it in this condition, we were both wounded in a way a few new boards and some nails wouldn't heal.

CHAPTER 4
DAHLIA

This was my fault. The destruction that lay around us. The furious agony on Frey's face. The dark frown Fen wore when he shifted back to human.

Rather than blinking us all to the room where Frey had put all the guests, we walked. I suspected it was mostly to give him time to collect his thoughts.

We stepped in the room to find the sleeping patrons waking up slowly, and the conscious ones looking perplexed.

"What the fuck is going on?" The ifrit demanded to know the instant we walked into the room.

"Curious to know that myself," Pan muttered from where he stood next to me.

I liked him. He was fun, in a big-brother kind of way. And not the *big brothers* I had at TOM, who were as likely break or fuck us—frequently both—as to actually help us learn and grow.

Frey opened his mouth, and audible bedlam broke out, with everyone talking over each other, shouting, and demanding answers.

"*Shut it.*" Fen's roar carried over it all.

That'd be sexy if his fury weren't tangible. If my guilt weren't gnawing at me from the inside out. This happened because I saved Minato. Because I walked away from TOM. Because I thought this was a good place to hide.

Because I couldn't clean up my own messes.

"We've been targeted by a Baku," Frey explained. "I thought the wards were stronger here at NEON, and I've failed you all. I beg your forgiveness, and the club has been closed until further notice."

No.

Fen grasped my hand before I could open my mouth.

But Frey shouldn't be the one apologizing or paying this price,

The end to the night was anticlimactic as the patrons offered their sympathy. Given they'd destroyed his club, even though they were dreaming at the time, Fen was quick to remind them they were lucky he'd let them live, and that Frey didn't want vengeance. They were guests in this realm.

I tuned out at the rumble of murmurs that rolled around the room again. Most everyone was sympathetic and impressed Frey found a way to deal with the problem. No one knew of a better way to take on the threat we had.

Pan gave me a long bow and tipped an invisible hat. "Pleasure meeting you, new dragon. I hope next time we run into each other, I'm more pleasant."

"I'm sure you will be." I gave him a smile.

Fen's growl was low, rumbling from his chest as more of a sensation than a sound.

Pan stepped toward the door. He paused and faced us again. "I've never seen anyone fight a Baku that way before."

"You've got a lot of experience with them?" Frey asked flatly.

Pan shrugged. "Not so much these days, but centuries ago I encountered a couple. Most of them are dead, so there's not a lot of opportunity for taking them on these days. In fact, I thought they were all gone."

"New dragons, new Baku, haven't you heard? The world is full of new and potential immortals." I couldn't keep the sarcasm from my voice. Those potentials, those ascended beings, were the reason TOM existed. The reason we'd been sent to hunt Minato. The reason Vidar fucked a dragon about thirty years ago, to hopefully make something like me.

Pan's cheer vanished, and seriousness replaced it. "I've heard. New immortals everywhere. If I remember anything about Baku, I'll call." He winked at me, but the gesture was forced. "See you around, baby dragon."

It was so ridiculous, so out of place, I couldn't help but laugh, though there was no humor in the reaction.

Pan walked out when Fen's upper lip peeled up.

Then it was just the three of us. "I'm sorry," I said softly. "Now will you let me go after her?"

"Not until we know how to fight her as more than a reaction." Frey sank onto a nearby couch and dropped his head into his hands.

Did he feel the club's destruction physically? This place was him. It was his realm. His pain had to be more than emotional.

"She wasn't supposed to be able to find NEON." I wasn't helping, but I couldn't take the words back. They were meant to reassure me, to let me tell myself this wasn't my fault.

It didn't work.

"Someone let her in. Someone broke my wards." Frey's voice was muffled.

"Vidar?" I hated saying his name. Especially knowing now that he was my father. That he was pursuing me because I could destroy what he'd built.

Fen clasped my fingers and tugged me closer as he rested his hand on Frey's shoulder. "Most likely," Fen said.

"No. Someone on the inside." Frey's voice was heavy.

His words hit me hard. He meant someone working for him. The way Minato had been. Another potential I hadn't recognized. A god we didn't know. A new TOM trainee. The possibilities were a mile long.

I had to make this right. I had to be worth something more than being a baby immortal who needed more protecting than anyone around me. I was a fucking dragon, and I was still— "I'll call Artura." At least that was something I could do. "See if she knows anything."

Frey's nod was almost imperceptible, but his silence spoke volumes.

Fen pressed his lips to my forehead. "Stay safe. Don't blame yourself."

"I'm not—" I couldn't lie about that. I totally thought this was my fault. "I'll be careful."

He rested a finger under my chin and tilted my head up to meet his gaze. "You are blaming yourself, because I would be." He brushed a kiss across my mouth. "Come back to us. We'll clean up here."

I nodded and stepped from the room to call Artura.

"Hello?" When she answered, she sounded curious, as if she hadn't expected a call.

Normal for most people, but not for a creature

older than humanity who had countless visions of the future. "Hi. It's Dahlia."

"Hello," Artura repeated. "What can I help you with?"

"You mean you don't already know?" It was meant to be a teasing question, but it came out with an unintentional edge. Not that I thought Artura did *teasing*.

Her silence made me think she'd noticed. "I don't. No."

I'd make polite small talk, but that had yet to be my relationship with Artura. Each time we spoke, she reminded me she was here to pass knowledge to me, and not to banter about how she was today. *Today* didn't matter in the grand scheme of things anyway, as far as she was concerned.

I hope I never reached the point where I couldn't appreciate something as simple as a day. "Do you know anything about Baku?"

"Yes. But only because I've done a lot of research since I helped fight the one holding you captive."

I was a little bummed I'd missed out on research, but Artura probably had ancient ways of looking things up that even made that not fun. "May I visit? Glean your knowledge?" It had taken a while for me to get used to how everyone deferred to her and her sister, Urd, but I understood now. They were ancient beings, and when I'd lived as long as they had, done the things they'd done, I'd want respect too.

Maybe not to be worshiped as something better than a god, but still...

"I'd enjoy your company, niece. You will find me in my bookstore."

"Thank you. I'll be there in a few minutes." I had one thing I needed to do first.

I returned to the lounge to find Frey and Fen speaking quietly and wearing matching deep frowns. "I'm going to talk to Artura. See what she knows. Before I go—"

"You're going to get dressed?" Fen asked, one eyebrow raised and an almost-smirk in place.

I looked down at the frilly panties and pasties I wore, with nothing on top. "Right. Good call. But also... I need what you have on Minato." I realized this wasn't an ideal time for anything except mourning, but I also knew they would want to act as much as I did. More.

Frey scrubbed his face. "It's not an exact location, but an idea."

"Okay." I could work with that. "We'll plug it into my program and let it work." I'd written a piece of software that was somehow imbued with magic I didn't know back then I had, that could scan the world for certain types of immortals and potentials. It worked a lot better if it had a starting point, though. "Let me get some clothes and my laptop."

Fen grabbed my arm as I turned away, his grip

rough. "If it finds something, you don't go without us. Without information on how to fight her."

"Of course not." As much as I'd love to be tough and strong and independent, I wasn't the girl who would go chase the bad guy alone. Movies and TOM had taught me an important lesson, from two very different perspectives—never go alone.

I blinked upstairs to dress and grab my computer. After taking enough of a shower to wash off the body glitter and blood, and tugging on some leggings, a skirt, and a black T-shirt, I was back in the lounge, adding Frey's information to my search parameters.

The program would run on the cloud, so the computer didn't need to stay up. I shoved it into my purse—a wonderful, magical gift from Frey a few years back, that was an actual bag of holding. I could keep anything in it. "I'll be back."

"Travel safe." Fen caught my face between his palms and brushed his lips over my cheeks, my nose, and finally my mouth.

"I will." I looked at Frey—god of lust and love, currently broken like his club—and stepped closer. I draped my arms around his neck, letting desire fill me until it poured over frustration and hurt and rage. Until it almost silenced everything else.

I pressed my body to his, offering my lust as a tribute to soothe him. "I'm sorry. We'll fix this."

"I know." He wrapped an arm around my waist and pressed his forehead to mine.

I swore the need I'd summoned for him pulsed and grew rather than waning. It surged so strongly, the physical sensation was nearly orgasmic. The feeling faded when he let me go.

"Thank you," he said.

I nodded and stepped away. The exchange was all about power, as in, feeding his. There was nothing more to it than there had ever been between us.

Still, an ache tugged at my heart as I blinked out of the room to take myself to Spain.

CHAPTER 5

DAHLIA

I appeared on a sidewalk in Spain, in front of a bookstore with *The Dragon's Hoarde* written on the sign. The sun was cresting the buildings, people milled around me like I'd always been there, and the general mood in the air was hurried-but-status-quo.

It felt wrong. It was likely not a single one of these people knew this store actually belonged to a dragon. None of them cared that gods and shifters and ancient warriors walked among them.

All of them just wanted to get to their next destination. Itched to check their social media. Were thinking about an upcoming meeting, or lunch, or if they had a text from their secret lover.

Resentment bubbled up inside me. I'd never had a chance to be *that*. TOM taught me gods were real before I hit puberty. They taught me to watch everyone. Everything. To suspect the world at all times.

And yet, Minato had gotten past my defenses again. And again. Made me think she was an ally. Made me believe Magnus was dead. Tried to destroy my world.

I stashed the thoughts in the little locked box of *don't open until never* in the back of my mind, and stepped into Artura's bookstore.

An unwelcome calm blanketed me. I may not want to hold onto the details of my past, but I didn't want to lose my anger with Minato. With myself. But being here, the atmosphere, the magic in the air, the endless rows of bookshelves that shifted their content and shape to each person who entered the aisles.

Not *home* the way NEON was, though. The thought was enough for me to rediscover that need for vengeance.

The woman behind the counter was petite, with white hair that hung down to her waist. She wore a sundress and looked deceptively young.

"Good morning." Artura greeted me with a pleasant smile. There was no warmth in her eyes, but there rarely was, so I wasn't hurt. She was kind, and that was fine. "I have coffee and cookies, if you'd like."

I managed a smile. "This is why you're my favorite aunt."

She rolled her eyes. "Don't lie to me, child. It's not flattering."

It wasn't a complete lie—cookies and coffee could get me to do a lot of things. But Artura was right that I wouldn't like Urd even if she bribed me with goodies. Partly because I'd been raised to believe Urd was solely responsible for all the prophecies that caused us grief. But even knowing better, I still resented that she'd let her name be attached to it all. I followed Artura toward the back of the shop, to a cozy sitting room tucked behind a discreet door.

After coffee was poured, along with generous helpings of cream and sugar in mine, we settled into the kind of flowered chairs that I'd only ever seen otherwise in old TV shows.

"If you're asking about Baku, does this mean that Minato is still a problem?" Artura asked.

Was she yanking my chain? Anyone else and I might wonder if she was asking to see my reaction, but I'd never seen any indication Artura was like that. Yes, she spoke in riddles, and she assumed the rest of the world had the same knowledge she did, but she didn't pretend not to know things.

But... "You've been researching her kind. Didn't you see her coming back?"

Artura hesitated. Weird. She sighed. "No. I assumed she would, but I haven't seen her in the future or now."

"Does that mean we win? That her destiny is

over soon?" And if so, was I more relieved, or jealous that she got to remove *fate wants my life* from her list of curses?

"I don't know. Possibly, but unlikely. She's like your friend, Magnus."

Oh. This had been explained to me before, and I'd discovered it to be true in the steps I took to control my own powers. Some people were hidden from a dragon's visions. "You've seen an absence though." Whatever magic gave us our power could hide certain beings, like Magnus, but it couldn't remove them completely. It blanked them out, more like a movie censor gone nuts with their black boxes.

"I see a lot of absences." Artura sipped her coffee. "Magnus is one of them, but you'll meet many in your life. If there's no point of reference, it's hard to tell who they are. In your case, a blank void could be Magnus. It could be Minato. It could be someone I haven't met yet."

Point of reference. "But I wouldn't be fighting Magnus."

"And if the person you're struggling with is also a blank spot in the vision, the instigator, I don't see the vision at all. You should've experienced this many times by now."

I had. But something kept me from telling her that, and I wasn't sure why. "Hmm."

"In fact..." Artura studied me. "It's odd that

you're confused by what I have and haven't seen. With my sisters, there was always a lot of overlap."

I shrugged. "Maybe that other stuff isn't important. If it is, you would've called me." I knew the instant I said it, that I was wrong. Artura wasn't a proactive visioneer.

The way she watched me now...

Fuck. "Okay, I know something big is coming." I'd seen multiple scenarios play out, and give the context, I knew they would happen soon. I refused to cling to the thoughts once I wrote each vision down though.

"Ignoring what you see is not the same as control." Now there was chiding in Artura's words.

I didn't care for that. "Choosing when I act on what I see *is* control. It's the same type you've been exercising for centuries."

"No." The saucers and coffee cups disappeared from both my hands and hers and reappeared on the table between us. "Close your eyes."

"Just tell me about fighting Baku." I hardened my voice.

"Do this for me first. It's a simple request on my part—you're asking me for help, and I would like something small in return. Close your eyes."

A bubble of fear grew inside, and I popped it, letting fear fall like glitter around my heart. What was I hiding from? I did what she said.

"Now stop fighting it."

Great advice. Thanks. I knew exactly how to do this, but letting her drive things might help me get answers more quickly.

I loosened my mental grasp on the wall I tucked so many of my thoughts behind. Was it possible I could see something happy?

The familiar clarity of thoughts that weren't quite mine pushed at my mind. Letting the images in were instinct at this point, and I relaxed just enough to let a little—

I was in a void, with no setting or shape. That didn't mean what I was seeing would take place in a similar environment, but it might. This was one reason the visions weren't reliable.

Nico was here—Magnus had been looking for him and was so sad she hadn't found him yet—but this wasn't the Nico I'd met. This man was in battered leathers—a modern day armor—and his facial features were sharper. More bird-like.

I was in the vision as well, and so was Fen. We were fighting something we couldn't see. Minato. Something else. It was impossible to tell. I couldn't see Magnus either, but that didn't mean she wasn't here.

A wound appeared on Nico's shoulder, inflicted by a weapon I couldn't see, and he crumbled in a wash of blood and pain.

The absence of sound was as loud as any scream that should have been there, and my eyes flew open.

"Nico." The word gasped past my lips. It took me a moment to focus on reality. To place myself back in Artura's back room.

"Nico... demus?" She studied me with a furrowed brow.

What the...? "Yes? Did you see him in your visions? Do you know him? he's a phoenix." *He promised Magnus he'd be back after dying. He's not yet. She'll be upset if he dies again.* I kept the more personal stuff to myself.

Artura's expression flicked to impassive in a blink. "No. I haven't had those visions." That felt like the truth. "There are no phoenixes left, and there aren't supposed to ever be again." That was a lie.

I felt it in every inch of me. She was hiding something.

"What do you know about Nicodemus? About Phoenixes?" If I could bring Magnus answers... I missed my friend, even though she was back. I hated seeing her so lost.

"That's not why you're here."

I didn't try to hide my growl of frustration. "You made me poke around in my head. In those stupid fucking visions. He's who I saw. Who is he?"

Artura's nostrils flared and her presence seemed to fill the room, though she remained the same size.

I was unimpressed.

"You can choose. I'll tell you how to defeat a

Baku, or what little I know about Phoenixes. You can't have both," Artura said.

Really?

I hated the ultimatum. I wanted to push until she gave me all the information I wanted, but that had never worked before. "That doesn't make me want to know the answers to both questions any less. It makes me more curious, and I will find both answers."

"I'm sure you will. But not from me."

Other people knew about Nico. No one we talked to knew anything about Baku.

I'm sorry, Magnus. "Tell me about how to defeat Minato."

A book appeared on the table between us, open to the middle. They'd taught us several languages at TOM, and I'd learned them all.

I didn't know how to interpret the combination of pictographs and lines. "What is that?"

"Old enough it doesn't have a name." Artura leaned in. "There are three relics that are said to be crucial in fighting a Baku." As she spoke, she pointed at different points on the page. "A diadem, a locket, and a sword."

What?

No.

I stared at her in disbelief.

"What don't you like now?" Artura stared back.

"That's not how you defeat a Baku, that's the final Harry Potter book."

The confusion on Artura's face looked forced.

She was still keeping things from me.

"I thought you were going to tell me how to deal with a Baku." Why did I think coming here was a good idea? Why did I think she'd give me any answers that I didn't claw out of the dirt myself first?

"And I have. I don't know where the relics are stored, but there are ways to find them."

I nodded. "Okay. And then once all the horcruxes are destroyed, we can beat he who shall not be named."

"This has nothing to do with horcruxes."

I blew out a puff of frustration. "Uh-huh. Thanks for nothing."

CHAPTER 6

FREYR

Fen and I worked in mostly silence as we made our way through the tattered remains of the NEON main room. I wanted to sweep up the entire area in one giant wash of magic, and send it into the void, so I wouldn't have to look at it anymore.

At the same time, I needed to examine each piece. Not only to determine if it was salvageable, but because nearly every single chair and table in here came from *somewhere*. They all had memories attached to them.

I brushed my hand over the back of a chair, and images flashed through my mind. A woman in a black tutu, over purple striped leggings, with combat boots and a T-shirt that said *Hackers do it with their fingers* was sitting in this chair. Just a few years ago.

Dahlia was here, pretending she wanted a job. Watching the dancers, chatting me up with nervous conversation.

This was where she sat the first time I met her. And now it was in splinters. Nothing but a back and a few legs remained.

A bubble of fury rose in my chest, and I forced it to dissipate.

Some of the tables had names scratched in them, and several of those were from immortals. The berserker, Davyn, when he thought he'd lost his destiny nearly a decade ago. One that looked like it was from tonight. My Greek was rusty, but the ornate letters obviously spelled *Pan*.

I paused on a scorched piece of tabletop and couldn't suppress this round of memories. When we'd opened the club, more than a century ago, it hadn't been called NEON. The themes had been different, the look was modern for its time, but some of the settings hadn't changed.

And this was the table Fen took me on, to make the club ours. To dedicate it to me. No one took control when I was fucking except me. Unless I was with Fen. My heart. My wolf. And he'd fucked me on this table, in front of a room full of gods and immortals, to make this place ours. To make this realm *mine*.

Now it was gone. The rage surged again, blackness seeping into my thoughts. A kind of anger I'd rarely experienced in my existence.

After so many centuries, I knew how to control a bad mood—even a godly one—but it was difficult to find the desire to beat this back.

My fingers brushed another splintered chair, and a new sensation tickled my thoughts. This wasn't a memory, it was foreign magic. It was... Vidar? Minato? A strange blend.

"What is it?" Fen asked.

I held up the support bar from a chair back. "I need the rest of this seat. Or at least more of it."

He nodded, and picked through a few nearby stacks of tinder, expanding his search as I did, until we found a seat with two legs attached several meters away.

"She was here." Now that I was holding the object, Minato's unique magic practically dripped from the oak. There was the fury again. She'd walked into my club. She'd been here and I didn't notice.

She couldn't mask herself from me with her own magic, but she'd been working with Vidar, and he had access to a lot. He could imbue already magical artifacts with more. For instance, adding sacrificed fae blood to a dragon's gift. The combination of magics on such an object could give anyone—even a mortal—access to similar magic.

I tighten my fist until splinters dug into my palm.

"Stop." Fen's calm voice penetrated the haze.

I breathed deep and forced myself to calm down. "I feel more in this. It's faint, like what Magnus is wearing when she comes back from waiting for Nico."

"Has she been sitting there recently?" Fen asked.

No. Magnus left to go find Nico overnight, and during the day she slept in her apartment. Sometimes she spent a few hours with Dahlia.

"This is different. There are no traces of Magnus, but the magic from that small town is here. Something besides her is there." Which made sense—If Nico was from there, it was likely he wasn't the only magic that called it home. "But what does it have to do with Minato?"

"I can go. Look around," Fen said. "Now, while no one expects us to be doing anything."

It was a good idea. "We'll both go."

"No." Fen was forceful but kind in that single syllable. "Drop me off, but you stay here and mourn. You need to do that."

I did. "Thank you. Stay safe."

I dropped Fen at the other end of the town from where Magnus waited, and he promised to call me when he'd finished looking around.

With him gone, solitude filled my soul. This would be a good respite. I could focus, find my center, find the shattered threads of my wards, and start to rebuild them.

I stood in the middle of the club, only half the debris gone, and closed my eyes. If I focused, I could feel those strands of broken web. The magic that made NEON safe, and the gaping hole in the middle.

Anger later. Rebuild now. I reached for the power and tugged. Weaving a new shield into the old was the same idea as using starter from an old, trusted wine, to build a new batch. I mixed the original with the fresh, whisking, intertwining, fermenting, all in millisecond increments.

The mixture soured as I worked, until I was encased in a foul, rancid magic shell that wobbled from the slightest poke.

My own growl startled me. I yanked all the new wards down and let the wisps float into nothing. My anger and frustration surged back, potent and cloying. Things weren't supposed to be this way.

The aura in the room twisted into a new shape. Dahlia was back.

"Oh. My. Fuck." She announced herself with a melodramatic frustration that had to be exaggerated, and was completely her. "All of that for nothing." She set her bag down on a nearby table with a huff.

The way she held herself, the way she spoke, it was easy to see the sexy, smart woman Fen loved. The creature who wanted to take on the world, though she was barely over thirty.

It was also easy to see her lack of experience.

Frequently charming, but today it made my frustration flare.

"She was going on about diadems and swords and lockets and... seriously?" Dahlia sighed, and finally looked at me. "How's it going here?"

The light switch to sympathy, the fact that it took her so long to get there after her arrival, shoved me into the fury I'd been struggling with since the fight ended. Why couldn't she just listen sometimes? Why did she always have to assume the world was against her?

I knew the answers, but I wasn't in the mood to be reasonable. I was tired of always being the one who understood. My club was in tatters. My realm. Someone might as well have stabbed me in the gut hundreds of times and left me for dead.

"The wards are still down." Dahlia sounded concerned now. "Do you want help putting them back up?"

Impudent little brat. Offering as if it were nothing, to replace the shields on this place. As if I hadn't built them using centuries of experience.

"No." I didn't try to hold back any of the power in my voice. "I want something else." I wanted to heal. I wanted to fuck. I wanted to dive headfirst into who I was, and drive home with her the reminder of the same.

I stalked toward Dahlia, and she stared back, eyes-wide, and a dark, muted lust whispering from her. What I did next would determine how this all unfolded. I could nudge those feelings of hers—use magic to draw them out—but I wanted her to go into this of her own accord.

So I took another step toward her. One of the fascinating things about Dahlia was she grew more defiant the more she was pushed. She was casual, flexible, willing to go along with most things or hide from the things she didn't like, unless someone told her *no*. Then she pushed back hard.

I didn't want to manipulate her, but it would be so easy to tell her she couldn't help. That she couldn't even fuck my pain away. That would get me what I wanted when she felt the need to prove me wrong.

And I wasn't going to do it. I'd nudge her defiance, but I wouldn't send it running off a cliff.

"What can I do?" Dahlia's voice quavered.

I gave her a wicked grin, walking forward as she moved back, until the wall stopped her. "If things hadn't fallen apart after your dance tonight, you know what I would've asked for." My anger surged again, freshly slashed with memories of NEON being destroyed.

I dipped my mouth near her ear. "I'll give you one guess what I want."

Her desire pulsed, tainted with a delicious fear. "What if I guess wrong?"

"I'll have to punish you." I dragged a finger down

her breastbone, over her shirt, pressing in enough to make my point but not to hurt.

"Then you want... ice cream?" Her playful tone didn't matter. It was what lay underneath that I was hungry for. The want. The heat. The desire to be used. All of it wrapped up in that same inability to take things seriously that was adding to my fury.

I pressed a hand to her throat and nipped her earlobe. "Wrong answer. How am I going to punish you?"

Her pulse hammered under my thumb. She licked her lips, and her breath came in shallow bursts. "Oh no." She was flowing with need. "You might have to hurt me."

I just might.

CHAPTER 7
DAHLIA

As a teenager, as a part of training, sex was a tool. A weapon. A form of currency. We were taught that other people had strong feelings around it, but that we never should. That wielding it was the same as drawing a knife or brandishing a credit card.

But Frey had taught me sex was so much more. The way he stalked me now, sex was an outlet. A way for me to lose myself in the fear and frustration of the last several hours, but be safe. A way for him to heal.

A guaranteed path toward some incredible fucking orgasms.

So when he backed me against the wall and promised punishment, nothing sounded better. He pressed his palm to my throat. His grip was rough and his kisses were mixed with bites along my lips.

This was a kind of intensity and fury I was used to from Fen, but not Frey.

The feeling mingled with my own frustration at the failed trip to Artura's, and scorched everything away but *now*.

The grunt Frey made was almost primal as he spun me, and tore down the back of my shirt. The sound of tearing, the burn on my skin, were delicious. As he sandwiched me between him and the wall, his restraint was gone.

He teased a rough touch up my chest to my breasts. There was a fast franticness in his movements that lit my senses on fire and drew my need to the surface. He rolled my nipples between his fingers, pinching and tugging, while he sucked and bit along my neck and shoulders.

Desire pulsed between my thighs, and squeezing my legs together only made the throb more insistent. This was a unique kind of torture. The kind I wanted to last forever, but also needed a conclusion to, in the form of the orgasm I knew was on its way. The combination of touches and sounds pounded in my veins and made my heart hammer against my ribs.

Frey turned my knobs and pushed my buttons until I was squirming and gasping with the need for more. He sank his teeth into my shoulder and dropped a hand between my legs. With each skilled, insistent press against my pussy, through my leggings, he drew me closer to orgasm, but he never let me tumble over the edge.

This was the kind of incredible pleasure that made my head swim. My whimpers fell out faster. Did he want verbal worship in exchange for an orgasm? Because I was happy to do that, always, but especially at this moment. "Oh, God, please."

"Please, what?" His deep voice rumbled through me, teasing every one of my senses with his power.

"Make me come the way only you can. I'll suck your cock. I'll let you use my body however you want. *God*, I need this. I need this from you." This was about more than filthy words—it would feed him and he'd reward me in return.

Frey's chuckle was like an invisible hand, stroking the coals of heat in my core. He ripped my leggings at the crotch and shoved my panties aside. When he slid two fingers inside me, abruptly and without pause, it stole my breath.

I was so slick, there was little friction. He pumped inside me, harder, faster, before sliding out of me and gliding his touch up to my clit. It didn't take much to make me come, screaming his name. Praying for more. Digging my fingers into the wall until they ached.

Frey didn't ease off. He bit the edge of my ear and ground his erection into one ass cheek. His touch was almost too much. I needed him to keep going, though.

Want. It was all I knew. I didn't know what words tumbled past my lips as my thoughts sank into pleasure. I was breathless and begging him. To make me come again. To bestow me with his gift. To mark me as his favorite above all other humans.

Did I really just say that?

He caught my earlobe between his teeth and tugged hard enough to ache. "You're not human, dragon. And there is no one else like you."

Another orgasm burst through me, and I was drowning in the sensation. He drove his cock inside me hard and fast at the peak of ecstasy, stretching me out. Making my body feel *more*. His fingers, slick with my juices, were on my throat again, squeezing, and yanking me into him while he fucked me with abandon.

The edges of my vision blurred with the onslaught of so many sensations. My head fuzzed. Floated. Where did I end and he begin? I never wanted this to be over.

I was pretty sure I came again, that I heard and felt him climax as well, but it was all one big pleasure-blur.

The intensity slid toward tenderness, as Frey slowed and stopped pounding inside me. His mouth along my shoulder became tender kisses instead of hungry bites.

As he lowered us both to the floor, he pulled me into his lap. The way he wrapped his arms around me, the safety and softness, helped me hold onto the lingering high.

That was incredible. But a sliver of me was terrified. Frey didn't do this. He didn't lose control.

Ridiculous thought. He hadn't this time either. He'd been in control the entire time.

Hadn't he?

CHAPTER 8

FENRIR

The little coastal town Frey deposited me in was exactly like Dahlia had described. A village frozen in time, despite the world going on around it.

Supposedly when Nico came back, he'd still be himself. Same age. Same appearance. Phoenixes just poofed into existence from beyond the grave, or something.

I could become a variable size and shape of wolf by sheer force of will, so who was I to question the way these magics worked?

Right before Frey left me here, he told me he didn't know what I should be looking for, but it was possible I'd recognize it when I saw it.

Sure. That might as well happen.

As I strolled down a cobblestone street, one- and two-story stone structures rising around me, the only thing I recognized was the calm in the air. It was non-threatening. It made me feel guilty for being here in a soothing place while Frey dealt with NEON.

I also knew he needed that. If I were in his shoes, I'd require the same—solitude. Mourning.

A breeze rushed around me, carrying the scents of meat, spices, and laughter from the other side of the village. Maybe I could go investigate in that directi—

My wolf growled in my head, and the hair on the back of my neck stood on end. What was that? Something in the air had changed. There was a threat, and I didn't know where it was coming from.

My entire body was instantly on alert, as I stepped closer to the buildings, to have a wall at my back, and scanned the street. Nothing—no one— here looked like a threat, but that didn't mean they weren't. Children played tag a few streets over. A woman whistled one story up, in the next building, as she dusted the room she was in, while another talked too loudly to someone about her investments overseas.

A door nearby clicked open, and my wolf snarled. My focus narrowed, not blocking the rest out, but making it less of a priority as I focused on that home.

Though I'd only met him a couple of times, I recognized Nicodemus the instant he stepped onto the front walk of the tiny cottage. The air around him, his mood, his posture, everything about him was pleasantly neutral.

But my wolf was growling and nipping at my thoughts to be let out.

I wouldn't do that, but since I didn't have another direction to search in, following him seemed like a good plan for now. There was no harm in observing.

Whatever it was about him or his presence that put my senses on high-alert, the feeling hadn't been there the last two times I met him. Perhaps it was because he was recently reborn. This almost tasted like death, unwilling and cloying.

Whatever it was, I hung back a few blocks as he strolled through town. He didn't move like a man who was in distress or looking to cause the same. His gait was casual, and the few times someone called his name, he smiled easily and waved.

Though his greetings were a little off. Not in a malicious way. More like he was... confused?

Odd.

Then again, I wasn't a master of most emotions. I knew *kill* and *fuck* and *don't touch the people I fuck or I'll kill.*

As we moved across the village, toward the scents that caught my attention earlier, a head of wavy auburn hair caught my attention. *Magnus.*

She was more observant than anyone but Dahlia. A Valkyrie couldn't necessarily detect magic, but she recognized threats of any type. Would she pick up on something with Nico? She'd most want to know what was going on if she saw me.

I hung back as much as I could, while still watching both of them. Dahlia wouldn't forgive me if something happened to Magnus again. Ever, but especially so soon.

Nico walked toward her on the other side of the street, and then past her, without so much as a glance.

Odder.

When she called his name, he stopped and looked at her with that same furrowed brow and blank stare he'd given the people who called his name moments ago.

She, on the other hand, didn't hesitate. She threw her arms around his neck and greeted him with the kind of kiss I felt from where I watched. I might not be good at the feelings, but her joy and desire were so potent, they mingled with the cooking meat scent in the air.

He embraced her back, but who wouldn't with a kiss like that?

When they finally broke apart, she was grinning, and he was staring at her with that same perplexed look. "I think you've mistaken me for someone else, gorgeous." His accent was thick. "I don't know you, love."

Magnus's entire posture shifted. For a heartbeat,

her shoulders slumped, and then her stance changed to something fiercer. Ready to fight.

That I recognized. I tensed, prepared to join her in an instant if needed.

If Nico saw the change in her, he didn't physically react. Was he lying? How could he not remember her? He'd been infatuated with her the last time I spoke with him. It had barely been more than a week.

He had died since then, but coming back the way he did was supposed to include his memories. He was supposed to be the same.

"We met, a little over a month ago?" Magnus said. "You healed me, with your tears. Bragi called you." She spat the name. "We stayed with him. You watched while he helped me get access to my Valkyrie again." Her voice faltered. "You and I fell... Were falling... We were..."

Nico shook his head." It's a fantastic story, and I wish I could've experienced it with you, but I woke up in what I assume was my own bed, two days ago. I don't remember anything."

That made him a threat. Anyone with the kind of power to die and come back to life, who didn't know who his friends and enemies were... Had Vidar gotten to him? Had Nico managed to slip into NEON without us noticing?

"I'll help you remember. It's easy enough to start over, isn't it?" Magnus almost sounded desperate.

He gave her a faint smile. "I can't very well turn down a Valkyrie, can I? Especially such a gorgeous one."

Her shoulders slumped again.

"I'm sorry, I need to be somewhere." He brushed his fingers over his lips. "It was lovely meeting you." Like that, Nico was on his way. I needed to follow without Magnus seeing me.

Where did she go? She'd just vanished from view.

"You're the shittiest tail I've met in a long time." Magnus's voice came from behind me.

Busted.

She had a ring imbued with some of Dahlia's power that allowed her to do certain things a dragon could do. Like blink from one place to the next.

So much for following Nico. I turned to face her.

"Did Dahlia ask you to follow me? To check up on me?"

"No. She doesn't know—" *The club was attacked and your boyfriend who doesn't remember you is currently our main suspect.* I doubted that would go over well. "I was looking for someone, and it brought me here. Coincidence."

There are no coincidences.

The disbelief on Magnus's face implied she felt the same. "Did you find it?"

"I don't know."

"Great. Let's go home."

She touched me, and the village vanished, replaced with our apartment. She was nowhere to be seen.

I growled at the room.

"You're back." Frey's voice came from behind me.

"Yeah. Courtesy of Magnus." I could smell the sex in the air, and it mingled with soap. In the background, I heard the shower running.

It didn't bother me that Frey and Dahlia fucked while I was gone—we hadn't put many limits on the relationship between the three of us, and I didn't blame either of them for wanting the other.

What slid under my skin and gnawed at me was the lingering anger I tasted radiating from Frey. That wasn't him, and if he slid into it, if he embraced those feelings, it might destroy him.

CHAPTER 9
DAHLIA

In the bathroom, I wiped the steam from the mirror. Purple and black stared back at me from my reflection. In my hair, my eyes, and as I angled my body and traced my fingers over my skin, over the bruises from the sex.

I didn't have a problem with the marks. I knew Frey had been looking for angry outlet sex, and the fact that he used his magic to make the marks linger when I should've healed instantly was simply another piece of evidence. The experience was incredible, like always.

He and Fen used to be so gentle with me in the bedroom. When I was mortal. When I thought I knew how the world worked, but really had no idea. The fucking was rougher now. They both had less restraint.

Something about this felt different, though I

couldn't put my finger on what. Was it just the lingering stress from the intrusion into NEON? I wanted to believe that was it, but...

I shook the thought with no conclusion aside, and dressed.

When I headed into the living room, Fen was back. He and Frey stopped talking the moment I entered the room.

That wasn't obvious at all.

"What's up?" I asked.

Someone knocked before they could answer, and I frowned. It was rare they had visitors, and even rarer that they knocked, so odds were high it was Magnus. If this was my place, she'd walk in without warning, the way she had hundreds of times with my apartment at TOM.

She'd done that here once, and it happened to be while Fen, Frey, and I were fucking. Not as awkward as it would've been for some people, but enough to make her announce her arrival going forward.

Neither man moved to answer, which made my frown deepen, so I strode toward the front door. Sure enough, it was Magnus, and the instant she saw me, she walked into the room.

"What's wrong?" The discomfort crawling over me said something was definitely wrong.

She gave a quick shake of her head and looked between me and Frey. "You first. Why is NEON just *out there* in the open? Where did the wards go?"

She hadn't been downstairs yet.

"There was an attack." I hated saying the words. Hated being yanked back into that moment. Hated seeing the creases in Frey's and Fen's brows deepen at the words. "Minato got in." Saying it aloud made me ill. "She put everyone into nightmares and...it was bad."

"Gods, I'm sorry. What do you need me to do?"

I had no doubt she was thinking along the same lines as me with her offer. As in, *let's murder the bitch.*

"We've got it handled for now." The earlier edge was gone from Frey's voice and he'd returned to his normal, even-keel self. "Besides, you have news of your own."

Magnus gave a quick shake of her head. "Now doesn't feel like the time."

"But it's why you came over," Fen said.

How did he know that? Why wouldn't she just be stopping in to say *hi*? Come to think of it, she was back early.

Frey studied her. "She found Nico."

Which everyone knew but me, apparently. I pulled Magnus into a hug. "That's amazing. Isn't it? Why are you scowling if you found him?"

"He claims he doesn't remember her." With Fen chiming in, this was like watching a tennis match.

Why were they spilling her secrets?

"Nico *doesn't* remember me." Magnus stepped away from my hug. "And they know this because your puppy dog boyfriend was following me for some fucking reason."

I'd think she read my mind, finally giving me an answer, except what she was telling me didn't clear anything up. "Why were you following her?" I asked Fen.

"He was following a lingering trail of energy from downstairs. From whomever let Minato past our wards." The way Frey said it, the explanation sounded reasonable.

Except, "You don't think it's Nico, do you?"

Fen shrugged. "I don't know. That town is old magic, but he gives off a bad vibe. And I have a hard time believing he forgot Magnus."

"Yeah, well I don't like the sound of it either." Magnus huffed as she sank into a chair. "But I was standing right there. I looked him in the eye. I felt that awkward initial response when—" She tugged on a loose strand of hair. "When I kissed him. He doesn't know who I am." The sadness in her voice was heavy and contagious.

"I'm sorry. This may not help, but Artura said something that made me think we can find more information about him. About Phoenixes. There are answers out there. Maybe we can force her to give them to us." I needed to do *something*.

Magnus gave a brief shake of her head, and focused on me. "It sucks, but it's not as important as what happened here. I'm going to help whether you brush me off or not, so you might as well include me in your plans."

I wouldn't want it any other way, so when Frey said, "Fine," I was relieved.

"Dahlia did learn something from Artura," he added.

I what? "That's not what I told you. She gave me some Harry Potter bullshit. And don't tell me she's an ancient being not familiar with modern literature. She owns a bookstore, with current books on the shelves. She knows what Harry Potter is."

"Do you remember the story of The bride's quest?" Frey gave his attention to Fen. "The crown. The dagger. The amulet?"

"No." Fen looked stunned. "It can't be that obvious. I heard that story all the time when I was a boy."

"Which is probably why we didn't think of it," Frey said.

Fen nodded. "That and it's about curses, not dreams."

"One and the same if you never wake up." There was a heavy bitterness in Magnus's voice.

"Do you know what they're talking about?" I asked her. "What are you talking about?"

Frey twisted his face in thought. "There are so many variations on the story, but it's never presented as being about the dreams. They're more about the bride's love for the husband, and her cleverness in freeing him."

I pushed out a sigh. "Fill me in, someone?"

"Like Frey said, the details vary, but the basic idea is that a man and a woman fall in love," Fen said. "They marry, and he gifts her jewelry of some sort as part of that bond. Frequently a necklace. They're happy. They're in love. Until one day another woman comes along and tries to seduce him."

Fen wasn't exactly the best storyteller I'd come across, but I was willing to wait it out to hear how this all went down.

"He refuses, because he loves his bride, and the bride chases the witch off with the iron scythe she uses to harvest wheat. So the witch steals the husband away instead. The bride goes after them, scythe in hand, because it's the only weapon she has. The witch tells the bride *when he dreams of you, they're only nightmares. He doesn't want to be with you.* However the witch agrees to give the bride three last nights with her husband."

"What's the catch?" I asked. There was always a catch.

Fen raised an eyebrow. "I'm getting there. The first night, the bride visits her husband, but he sleeps, and she can't wake him. Worse, when she tries to wake him, he mumbles her name. He thrashes in his slumber and tells her to stay away. The second night, it's the same. Despairing, the bride wanders the witch's castle, searching her soul for a solution. It's then that she stumbles on the witch's secret room and her preparations to enter the husband's dreams."

"Wait. So the witch just lets the bride roam the castle and doesn't keep an eye on her?" I wasn't buying it.

Frey sighed. "It's a fairytale. It's a cautionary fable, not an intricately edited novel. It's going to have plot holes."

Great. More inconsistent than a dragon's prophecy. I kept the thought to myself. "I'm listening."

"Thank you." Fen gave me a brief nod. "The bride sees that the witch dons a crown of thorns, and has a short spell that she says along with it, that implies the crown will keep her grounded to the real world while she enters the husband's dreams.

"The moment she's certain the witch is asleep, the bride steals the crown, and goes to sleep next to her husband. When she wears the thorns, she bleeds, but the pain reminds her that she's real. The bride recites the words the witch did and enters her husband's dream. She finds another version of herself—the witch in her form—already there, tormenting her husband."

I had a good idea where the story was going at this point, but I wanted to hear Fen finish it, and if I interrupted he may not. Apparently he was a better storyteller than I gave him credit for.

Fen glanced at me, as if waiting, then continued when I didn't say anything. "In the dream, the husband doesn't know which woman to believe. Until the bride shows him the amulet he gifted her on their wedding night. She uses her bond to the waking world, the crown, to pull them both to consciousness. They go find the sleeping witch, decapitate her with the scythe, and go back home to live out the rest of their days happily."

Ah, fairy tales. Where kidnapping and homicide were just part of the day-to-day. When I heard stories like this, it drove home for me how much the gods had been influencing humanity for millennia.

"In other words," Frey said, "Artura was probably telling you the truth. If we find the three objects, we may have a chance of fighting Minato."

I did like the idea of cutting the witch's head off, but knowing the story still didn't tell us where to start looking.

CHAPTER 10
FREYR

My calm had returned, and the red haze of rage that had clouded my vision earlier seemed more like I'd imagined it. The release with Dahlia was healing, but I hated that I'd lost control to begin with. Whatever caused it, I needed to keep a tighter rein on my anger going forward.

"Then we agree there's likely something more to these stories," I said. "It's our only starting place."

Lines were etched in Magnus's brow, and the way she slumped in her seat was telling about her state of mind. "But Dahlia went all the way to Spain, and walked away without more information, because this all sounded too much like a book series?"

"Not quite." Pink dotted Dahlia's cheeks and her gaze was cast down. She reached into her bag and pulled out several books. "I took them anyway, because she was offering and I didn't know what else to do."

A direction. Finally.

Magnus huffed and grabbed the thickest book from Dahlia. "My love life may be in shambles, but at least this is something I can do. We're looking for hints about how to find and use these *magical items,* correct?"

I nodded my confirmation.

"Do we think we're looking for a scythe, or is it possible it's a dagger?" Fen asked.

Dahlia set the remaining books on the table, with the exception of one, and settled back with her selection. "Artura called it a sword, so I assume it could be anything. Why?"

I knew why, and I was surprised Fen was willing to bring it up. "Loki has a collection of one-handed blades. He prefers the easily concealable ones, and likes to brag that across his collection, he has the means to kill any immortal who crosses him."

Fen didn't like having contact with his immediate family. His uncles were fine, as was his grandfather. However, dealing with his father...

"Doesn't seem likely one of those is our answer, does it?" Magnus didn't look up from her book. "Doesn't that strike you as too easy?"

Without question.

"Loki used to brag—probably still does—that if

a blade wasn't in his collection, it either wasn't worthwhile or the original owner wasn't surrendering it. He also insisted he knew where any piece was that he didn't have," Fen said.

Dahlia opened her book and delicately turned through the first few pages. "We all know Loki's most likely to tell the truth when he thinks people won't believe him, don't we? And rumor is he's severed ties with TOM."

He'd been a member of the board with TOM, and she and Magnus were both familiar with his approach to things. But TOM wouldn't be helping him now and he wouldn't be harboring secrets on their behalf. But he would be worried about them hunting him.

Magnus held her place in her book with her finger, and half closed the pages. "Can we torture him as payback for what he did to the Nobles? I mean... *for information?*"

She struck me as being more bloodthirsty than normal today.

I understood her reasons, and that was something I shouldn't be able to say.

"Torture doesn't really... You know." Dahlia sounded apologetic.

Magnus shrugged. "Doesn't really work. Yeah. But a girl can dream. Fantasize. Create complex psychological alternate realities."

"Torture may not be effective, but Loki loves one thing above all else," Fen said.

I knew this answer too. "Himself."

"Talking about himself," Dahlia said.

"Saving himself," Magnus added.

It seemed as though we were all on the same page.

"If we can get him to talk about himself. His collection." Fen cracked his knuckles one at a time, the loud pops punctuating his each word.

It was an interesting approach, but it lacked as much detail as the rest of this plan. Were we right to focus on this one idea?

We did need a starting point. "Are you simply going to walk up to his front door and ask?"

Magnus gave a short nod, her lips pursed. "Yes."

"We'll tell him the truth. Or most of it." Dahlia set her book back on the stack, not having looked much at all. "We'll approach this the way he would, and let him believe that we know for a fact that after Vidar and Minato are done with us, Loki's the next target for betraying the board."

That seemed like a solid way to get him to take the dagger and go into hiding, if he had it.

"He's not going to work with us, and even if he does..." Fen trailed off.

I picked up the thought. "...that's not the kind of help we want."

"We don't expect him to work with us." Magnus set her book aside too, and stood.

"We expect the one piece in his collection that he thinks is the answer, to vanish."

Moments like this, it was clear why Dahlia and Magnus had been a team. They picked up each other's strategies without pause, and it was a thing of art to witness.

However, the number of holes in this plan concerned me. The next one being, how were we supposed to know if a piece vanished from Loki's collection? I opened my mouth to ask.

Dahlia smirked. "We'll pay him a visit." She talked over me, answering before I could ask. "Fen and I will. I'll give the room a glance, figure out the best place to leave a camera or two, then magic them in after we leave again."

"You're not going, I am." Magnus stepped forward, apparently no longer on the same page. "I'm his top student. I know all his tricks."

"You know all the tricks he taught you." I hated to be the one to shoot her down. This felt like a task she needed, and I wished I could move out of the way and let her have it. I didn't want anyone doing this, but someone who Loki might consider a protege seemed like the least good option. "And he knows everything he left out, and everything he taught you that was wrong."

The way Dahlia sighed, she expelled sorrow and

regret. Something else I shouldn't be able to feel. "I can't let you go," she said.

"You can if I'm the right person for the job." Magnus's scowl deepened. "Let me fucking *do* something."

Dahlia twisted her face into a deep frown.

"Dahlia is right. She and I need to be the ones to do this." The words sounded like they pained Fen to say. "I'd guess that Loki struggles with her unique brand of interrogation."

That was a fair point. Dahlia was a nervous talker, especially around people she didn't know or who intimidated her. In school, she'd learned how to turn that twitch into a way to extract information from people. Loki tended to be focused—to have a one-track mind—and that would make it difficult for him to follow Dahlia's tangents.

Logically, this entire thing made sense, aside from our initial reasons for starting with Loki. However, I was concerned about every aspect of our approach.

"Then the plan is to walk into the snake's den, tell him the woman I love is in danger, and so am I, and that we think he has the solution, and by the way, he's next?" The way Fen summed it all up didn't ease my concerns.

Dahlia gave a brief nod. "Yup. You be you. Say what you'd normally say, and I'll pick up the rest."

"How will you find him?" I wanted that to be the hole in their plan that they didn't have a solution for.

"I know where he is." Because of course Dahlia did. "My program keeps a running check of all TOM board members I've found."

Magnus's scowl twisted into something pained and angry. "Do you know where…?"

Dahlia shook her head, despite the incomplete question. "If I did, I'd have hunted him down and killed him for what he did to you. But he's vanished completely. More than before. The night Nico die—He's gone."

They were talking about Bragi.

An impassive mask slid onto Magnus's face, she returned to her seat, and grabbed her book again. "Go do this. Find us answers."

I wanted to tell Fen not to go. To stay and we'd find another way to hide. I wanted to tell Dahlia the same thing, but for different reasons.

And it was a request neither of them would listen to.

I couldn't shake the feeling of dread welling inside me. As Dahlia's favorite movie hero would say—Things were about to go sideways in the worst possible way.

CHAPTER 11

FENRIR

I hated this. This action felt like I was crawling home with my tail between my legs. True, I'd never seen this specific location, but it was Loki's abode, and I'd spent centuries avoiding this part of my family.

As we stood in front of the condo door, Dahlia squeezed my hand.

I was grateful she was here, as I knocked.

When Loki opened the door, he was already halfway through his sigh. "I can't fucking believe you found me."

"I never lost you," Dahlia said. "You just weren't important enough to let know."

Gods, I loved her.

If her words ruffled Loki's scales, he didn't let the reaction show. "I was important enough for you to keep track of, though."

"Incidental, I'm sure," I said.

He stepped aside and opened the door wider. "You might as well step inside the wards, in case there's any chance the actual threats looking for me haven't already seen where you are."

His appearance had changed from the last time I saw him. Then again, he tended to switch up looks every few decades. The golden hair and beard were a repeat, though. A throwback to the beginning of our lives. From a time when he was still *Dad* rather than another enemy.

I wasn't interested in small talk, and Dahlia did say I should be myself. A request I was grateful for. Directness suited me. "We're here about—"

"The blade." Loki already had another sigh ready for us, and handed me a sheathed dagger, handle toward me. "The Baku. The fact that Vidar wants you dead. Am I on the right track?" He glanced at Dahlia. "Rumor is you're a dragon."

She flexed her fingers inches from his face, and they shifted into her dragon claws. That was such a casual motion for her now, and the way she slid into it was enticing. "Rumor is true," she said.

Loki didn't flinch or back away. "I bet it pisses Vidar off to no end that out of all of those little bastard dragon babies, you were the one who hit the jackpot."

I growled a warning at the derision in his voice.

He raised an eyebrow in response. "Great. Let's

skip the interrogation part of this conversation, shall we?" The knife kills the Baku, but I don't know where the other pieces are. I have it in case she comes for me. Get to her first, and I won't have to worry about that. Fail, and the knife returns to my hand. As you kids say, *'Kay, thanks, byeeee.*"

"Just like that?" While I preferred direct, this was ridiculous coming from Loki. It was also not believable information in any way. I clipped the knife to my belt regardless. No reason to refuse an offered weapon from him if there was any chance it was a blade with an edge.

Loki shrugged. "I spin an elegant tale, and you'll call it bullshit. I give you a brief, short truth, and you assume I'm a liar. A guy can't win."

"A guy with a history of being a bullshitter."

He looked at me blankly. "I didn't expect *you* to believe me. I'm surprised you're even here. You believe that, don't you?"

I did.

"But you..." Loki faced Dahlia completely. The fact that he'd half turned his back to me was an insult that made my hackles rise. "You've already seen how this goes down, and you know I'm telling the truth."

"No." Dahlia shook her head.

Loki snorted in disbelief. "*No?* You're going to pretend that with the ability to see how all of this unfurls, the gift of literal prophecy, you can look and you haven't?"

This was typically where Dahlia faltered—when her heritage and the way she used her dragon gifts was called into question. When she mimicked Loki's snort, I hid my grin of satisfaction.

"You've been living for centuries based on the stories of three sisters," Dahlia said. "Making your every important decision based on what they told each other at the beginning of time, to keep from being bored. You're afraid of a little girl you've never met, because some stuffy old ancient texts told you that she might bring you to your knees. And you're going to mock me?"

Interesting approach—insulting him directly.

"You're supposed to be different from the other Nobles, but you're using the same techniques I taught all of you." Loki's tone slid toward disgust. "You should've just sent Magnus. She'd be more likely to join me in the bedroom anyway."

I grasped Dahlia's hand, and watched the rage splash across her face. Everything about this was off-kilter, making the hairs on the back of my neck stand up. When we arrived, I assumed the feeling was because of where we were, but this sensation matched the one I had around Nico. It was intense danger with no obviously connected threat.

"What are you up to?" I asked.

"I'm giving you the fucking knife, so you don't have to steal it later." Loki sounded exasperated.

I felt the tension quaking through Dahlia, and it mingled with the taste of death in the air. What was about to happen?

"Why?" My wolf nipped at the edges of my mind, whined to come out and fight.

The way Loki stood in the midst of it all, looking like his normal, unconcerned self, made the entire situation worse. If there was a threat, he should be reacting. "I told you why," he said. "Honestly there are decades I wonder if your mother lied about me being your baby daddy."

"Trust me—I've wished on many occasions for it to have been the mailman." I wasn't insulted by his words.

Some of Dahlia's tension lifted with her smirk.

"Great. Insults exchanged, you don't believe my story and I don't care. Bye." Like that, Loki's mood shifted again.

Dahlia cocked her head to one side. "You're in a massive hurry to get rid of us."

Loki's nostrils flared. "Yes. I am. *Go. Away.*"

"Maybe we should sit. Chat. You should be a polite host, and offer us tea and coffee. He's an ancient one." Dahlia nodded at me. "He deserves respect, regardless of what you think of me, and you're being rude."

The feeling of *danger* grew, as did my need to

fight. My wolf was howling. I didn't have a target, but it was about to become Loki, if I couldn't find another place to focus.

Wait. Clarity sank in bright and hot. If Loki was pushing for us to leave, did that mean he expected us to do the opposite, and stay? We needed to do what he was suggesting, and go now. The impulse was potent. "Dahlia." I reached for her.

She looked at me with confusion, then wavered on her feet. "What?" She wobbled some more, and pressed a hand to her forehead. *"No. No, no no."* Her voice dropped to a murmur.

I stepped between her and Loki, keeping one arm pressed into her in case she needed the physical support.

Loki stepped back. "I tried to get you to go." He vanished from the room.

The shout that ripped from Dahlia's throat was raw fury, and when I spun to face her, her unfocused gaze said she wasn't looking at anything in this room.

"Don't attack if you want her to wake up." Minato appeared next to Dahlia.

I let my growl roll loud and long, and tensed, ready to strike.

"Because what Frey did... I can make this outlast that." There was no fear in Minato's voice. "I can make sure she stays in this dream forever."

My wolf emerged, and I growled louder as I

searched for the best angle of attack. I was a fucking god and I could take Minato's head off. Make sure the wounds never healed and ensure that she stayed dead.

Could she make good on her threat as well? *What do you want?* I'd keep her talking. That was what Dahlia would do. Distract Minato so she couldn't act, and then attack her.

"For Vidar to kill you both." Minato dragged a finger down Dahlia's cheek, and the scream Dahlia let out chilled me to the core.

I bared my teeth and lunged.

CHAPTER 12

DAHLIA

I wanted to pretend I didn't recognize what was happening to me. It would be great if I could tell myself that the visions dancing around me, the scenes playing out like I was an invisible character in a 3D movie, weren't there.

But the practice I'd done over the last month, to hone my dragon visions, told me exactly what this was. I'd been sucked into an all-too-real scene, at one of the worst times possible.

Kirby sat on the ground a few meters away. Ash smudged her face, her hands, and her armor. Blood clung to her hair and clothing, though I couldn't tell if any of it was hers. She looked defeated. I hadn't seen Kirby wear that kind of surrender... ever.

She wasn't alone. Gwydion sat next to her. Aya. A woman I didn't recognize.

No, I did—Aya had shown Fen a picture. She was Astrid.

This was a nightmare. But not in the literal sense of it being a bad dream. Dragon visions felt different, even different than a waking dream. The colors were both surreal and hyper-real. This was a future playing out before my eyes.

The group were all friends as far as I knew, but not people who fought together. Their loss, whatever it was, radiated from them in waves.

Nothing about this scene was right. Kirby would never go into battle without Starkad. Neither of them would allow it. Gwydion would stand by her side, but he didn't fight, not anymore. He'd surrendered the magic to do so. And it wasn't that Starkad was a blank spot I couldn't see—there were none of those here.

It was my understanding that Astrid wasn't a fighter either. Not the stand-on-the-front-lines-of-war type. But she was dressed like a Valkyrie. The other women with them were Valkyries as well, in glorious armor, their wings drooping, and their expressions drawn.

Magnus wasn't among them. A blank spot that could be Magnus wasn't either. Why not?

Go away.

This vision was shitty and I wanted it gone. I could mutter *go away* in my head as many times as I wanted, even scream the words, but that wasn't working. This potential event was racing through my brain without my permission.

The group was talking, but I couldn't hear any words; the roar in my ears was too loud.

"...*should have...*" Kirby's voice was so soft, I was surprised it carried over the chaos of my mind. "...*been here...*" Could anyone hear her? She looked like she was muttering. How did I hear her? "...*she should've seen... Why didn't she warn us?*"

"She's not omniscient," Aya said. So someone was listening after all. "She doesn't pick and choose what to know."

Me?

Because I did. Every time I had a dragon vision, I chose not to let it impact how I reacted to the future.

"*She* did." Hurt dripped from Kirby's voice. Or sadness. Or disgust. I couldn't tell. Not that I should be able to. "It's all wrong. All of it." She looked up, and I swore her gaze met mine. "Why didn't you warn us?"

—the fuck?

This was a dragon vision. I was *positive*. They had a different feel to them than dreams or reality. I didn't want to see this, but now that I had, I couldn't shove the thoughts aside the way I normally did.

Was that Fen growling? He wasn't part of the vision. Or was he?

The world wobbled and changed. It wasn't obvi-ous, but more like the black cat walking across Neo's path twice in *The Matrix*. Things felt different, as though it had all been reset.

Kirby and the others were gone. I was in a cave. I'd been here before, when Vidar captured me and let Minato torture me. Everything was hyper-real. Sharp. Distinct. Too clean.

This was a dream. Minato.

The intensity sucked me in, even knowing what I was trapped in. Every bit of fear and anger I'd had the day she imprisoned me rushed back, and Fen was in front of me. So were Frey and Magnus. I was a dragon, and I had no control. I was as fierce as my aunts, slashing and tearing, destroying the people I loved and unable to stop.

I screamed at myself, but my voice didn't work. I pushed harder to make me stop killing.

Finally, a scream tore from my throat, reverberating off cave walls and shaking the ground.

It was too late. They all lay dead and tattered on the ground in front of me.

Fen growled again, but the sound didn't come from his body, it came from outside my head.

He wasn't dead after all, and I needed to get to him.

I could move freely in my dream, but my limbs felt like they were chained. As with my voice, I pushed and struggled, until my arm twitched. My leg kicked.

My eyes flew open and I was in Loki's again.

Minato stood next to me, and all of my instincts shifted to *kill*, especially seeing Fen as a wolf.

Minato's gaze met mine, and surprise splashed across her face before she blinked out of sight. Her voice echoed in my head. *Keep looking for me, and everyone you love will die by your hand.*

What the fuck was that?

"Dahlia." Fen was human again, standing in front of me, concern etched across his face. "Tell me you're all right, but also tell me you can get us out of here before we talk about the rest."

Because we were in Loki's apartment, which he was comfortable leaving us alone in, and nothing about our surroundings was safe. Forming the thoughts grounded me. I took Fen's hand. "This is all so fucked up." I blinked us back to the apartment.

When we appeared in the living room, Magnus and Frey were sitting, reading Artura's books. They both looked up.

"How did it—"

"What's wrong?" Magnus talked over Frey.

He raised an eyebrow, but his expression softened as he looked at me. "Problems?" He sounded concerned.

Fen held out the knife. "Loki insists this is the blade we want, so who knows what it is or isn't. But Minato was there. She pulled Dahlia into a dream."

Magnus bristled. "*What*? You don't just drop a bomb like that and pretend it's nothing." She pressed a hand to my cheek. "Are you still you? Are you dreaming?"

"No." I was furious that Minato had been there, and we hadn't been able to catch her. To stop her. But, "it started as a vision." I didn't want to talk about it, but it wasn't right for me to keep this one to myself. Describing it was almost as bad as living it—there was so much sorrow and terror. How many times would I have to see this one?

"Why wasn't I there?" Magnus was probably talking about both the vision and Loki's.

I shook my head. "I don't know. None of us were. The whole scene was wrong. Out of place."

"It could take place tomorrow or a thousand years from now," Frey said. "We don't know what will change between now and then. However, it seems more likely it was all Minato's doing."

They were focusing on the wrong thing, and I didn't know how to make them see otherwise. "Kirby looked right at me. She was so accusing. Whatever it is, I have to tell her. I have to stop it—"

"You have to stop. Period." Fen rested a hand on my arm. "Not being worried, but this isn't the time to react. We don't know if that was a vision."

"But it was, until Minato changed it." I was talking to three brick walls.

Magnus scrunched up her face. "Are you sure?"

When even she questioned me, I was in trouble. "I can tell the difference."

"Is that really the case?" Frey asked.

I swallowed back frustration filled with anger. "Yes. You want proof, you help me prove I know what I'm talking about. If you push away the passion Minato uses to make dreams vivid, and the vision is still there, that should tell us which parts were her."

Frey set his book gently on the coffee table, and crossed the room to me. "If it will put the matter to rest." He settled his hands on my cheeks, and closed his eyes. Heat flowed between us, quickly becoming icy. My anger faded. My frustration. My desire. Fear remained, but the rest was numb.

When Frey opened his eyes, a blank stare met me.

Creepy.

"Well?" His question was flat.

"The vision is still there. With Kirby and the others. The other..." The other what? I remembered describing the scene in the cave, but the images were out of reach, like forgetting a dream upon waking up. "Gone."

"You have your proof, are you happy?" Frey's question was abruptly sharp.

I wasn't sure how to respond. "Yes."

Fen frowned. "You should write this down," he said.

Nope. Nuh-uh. Not in a million bazillion years was I committing one of my dragon visions to a medium like *written word*. "Writing these things down is how shit starts. It's why TOM exists. FU. Nope. Not doing it."

"Not to share." Frey was almost as growly as Fen before a fight. What the hell? "You need to get the details right, while they're still fresh in your mind."

"He's right. The mind plays tricks, and the memory will shift and fade," Fen said.

It wouldn't. This was so vivid... And even if I forgot, or got bits wrong, would it matter? The details were already fading, and I had to act on it. If I was going to do that, I had to get the details right. "No one else can know I did this."

Frey's grunt was heavy and angry.

No, really, what happened?

"You never have to tell anyone outside of this room that it exists." As Fen spoke, a wisp of comfort flitted through me. Was he doing that?

I didn't want to feel better, but my mind was already rearranging itself into an order I could work from. Magnus took the book from Fen and stood. "Go write down your vision. If there's something out there about Nico... Maybe Brit remembers reading something."

Brit had read everything in the TOM library at school multiple times. She hadn't had answers before, but sometimes new questions jogged old thoughts.

Magnus headed to her apartment next door, and I headed into the home office to type in solitude.

I'd been up for more than a day. The lack of sleep didn't get to me the way it did a few months ago, but sometimes the exhaustion sank in, and as I sat in front of my laptop, every part of me was weary. I struggled to find that balance between grasping every detail before they all slipped away, not planting any of my own, and not falling into the emotions again.

The longer I worked, the heavier my limbs and eyelids felt.

And then I was reliving the vision, but not the way I had before. The scenery was warped. The people sounded wrong. Everything was like moving through molasses. Each time I tried to pinpoint a detail, to grasp it so I could record it, it changed.

Like a dream. A real one, not a Minato-induced one. The entire scene was ethereal and fleeting.

"Time to wake up." Fen's voice was gentle, as was the way he shook my shoulder.

Apparently falling asleep at my desk wasn't something that went away with achieving immortality. I straightened up, rolled my neck, and the ache vanished immediately.

Neat trick.

When Fen kneaded his fingers into the muscle anyway, and began to massage, I didn't argue. His strong grip, tender and attentive, was incredible. It drew me out of the lingering traces of fucked-up dream, and let me lean into his touch.

Where's Frey? The question died on my lips as I felt the magic in the air shift, grow stronger, and then shatter. "Frey's trying to put the wards back in place?"

"He is. Don't suppose you can tell if he's succeeding."

"He's not."

Fen kissed the top of my head. "Then he needs to focus. Let's not interrupt."

That sounded like a statement that had a plan behind it. "What did you have in mind instead?"

"Come spar with me." He glided a light touch down my arms to grab my hands, and tugged me to my feet.

In school, I hated sparring. I was weak, and it was an excuse for the others to beat me up.

Fen had taught me to enjoy the practice, though. Not only because I was powerful now, though that helped. He made it fun, rather than a chore or a punishment.

We headed to the door at the edge of the living room that Frey had put in place, which led to the perfect outdoor spot—a clearing on a small island in the middle of the Pacific.

I opened the door, and frowned at the blank wall that met us, rather than a sprawling beach. How very Winchester House, and also super disconcerting. Especially since this gate was partly my magic. I should've felt it when it shattered.

"It's all gone." Frey's flat voice came from behind us. "I had to tear down everything that connected us to NEON, to other places. None of it can be in place until I destroy it and rebuild it."

The news was disconcerting, but the heartbreak in his voice was devastating.

CHAPTER 13
FREYR

Destroy was a severe word, and I didn't want to sound melodramatic. I simply didn't see another solution. It didn't help that the anger was back, hammering in my skull. The feeling wasn't as potent as before, but it had slipped in shortly after Dahlia and Fen returned.

The way they were watching me now, the news was hitting them as hard as the decision had impacted me. The apartment floor we lived on had never been physically attached to NEON—our home was at the top of a skyscraper and the club was underground, beneath other buildings.

Now the connection was gone between the two. I needed to tear out the core structure of magic, to start again from scratch. It was the only way to figure out where the chips were in the foundation.

At least, that was what I told myself, and I had to

repeat it enough times to believe it. Using the old to rebuild hadn't worked, so nothing else made sense.

"Where are we, physically?" Dahlia asked.

The question surprised me. "You don't already know?" For someone so focused on having all the information, all the time, regardless of the detriment, how had she ignored this? For some reason the notion made my frustration grow.

Especially when she shrugged. "I never focused on it. You've got this Howl's Moving Castle thing going on, where any door could lead anywhere, and I just always figured the core wasn't as important as the fact that you kept us safe."

Ah.

In a way that helped me feel better, but there was always a pop culture reference with her. At least this time, it was grounded in an older story. Where was this fury coming from, that wanted to roar at her for being so... her? I didn't want that at all. "We're in Bangkok."

"Okay. I should tell Magnus, so she's not surprised if she decides to go out."

I expected Dahlia to walk next door, but she pulled out her phone instead.

"Something's bothering you." She kept her attention mostly on me while she tapped on the screen. "Fen and I are going to cheer you up."

That was something I definitely *didn't* need. I was surprised that Dahlia noticed, regardless. "You don't have to cheer me up. What I need is for you to stop being a child about so much of this, and start taking these threats seriously, so we can get our lives back."

The words came out with more venom than I intended, not that I should have spoken them at all, and Dahlia's instant hurt gnawed at me.

It also fed the anger, which I didn't care for.

"Hey." Fen's voice was hard, and he stepped between Dahlia and I. He gripped my chin, and forced my gaze to his.

Creation, if he took her side—

"This is more important right now." He searched my face. "*You* are most important right now. Whatever's going on—"

"Whatever's going on?" Rage trickled in. "We're being hunted." And grew as I spoke. "Our home is being dismantled piece by piece. Centuries of neutrality and security, safe haven for others, are gone, because—"

Fen crushed his mouth to mine. This wasn't a gentle kiss. It was hard and raw and a hint of fangs dug into my lips. He pressed in harder, as he slid his hand to my throat. We both stumbled back, until I collided with the wall, and still he devoured my grunts.

The connection was uncut passion. Desire flowing through me and seeping into the cracks. Filling in the fractures and forcing out the haze of red. This was real. This was love and desire. My fury was fleeting, and slipping away fast.

I moved my hands to Fen's neck, and tunneled my fingers in his hair, gripping tight. It shouldn't have been possible, but I deepened the kiss, falling into him. Into us.

"Do you want me to go?" Dahlia's uncertain question wove into the moment.

Glancing at her, I saw hints of vulnerability, and underneath that, a haunted look. She may be immortal now, but she could still be harmed. She had her soft, sweet moments, and seeing those traces now, made my desire surge hotter.

A light sigh slipped past my lips as Fen and I broke apart. So much better than a snarl.

"No." Fen glanced over his shoulder at her. "What I want you to do is go get those dice you got for your birthday."

No. Not that. Anything but that.

The protest died at the back of my throat, lodged in thoughts that were lightly anger-clouded.

The dice had been a gift from Min, who claimed he misunderstood when he heard Dahlia and Brit talking about *dice games*.

I suspected he knew exactly what they meant, given that he'd kept up with modern trends and technology despite being thousands of years old, and that he simply thought it would be funny to gift her the game. Gwydion may have had some part in the decision as well. There were times the pair acted as though they didn't have five-hundred-years experience between the two of them.

Dahlia looked between us. "Frey doesn't like those when he's *not* pissy."

"I'm not—" I snapped my jaw shut the instant I heard the edge in my words, and dragged in a deep breath through my nostrils. I had to trust Fen. "Go get them."

Dahlia didn't look convinced, but she headed into the bedroom anyway, and returned a moment later with a small box in her hand. The dice were a set of those novelty things that had body parts on one and actions on the other, and when put together, they were supposed to have erotic results.

I didn't understand why anyone needed a set of dice in order to decide how to lick, suck, or fuck another person. However, as we sat on the floor around the coffee table, I was willing to see how this played out if it meant dispelling the rest of this cloud that hung over me.

"What are the rules?" The game was made by elves—what fae became when they were cast out of their realm—and they tended to be particular about their rules.

Dahlia unfolded a single slip of paper and read from it. "Roll the dice. Pick a partner. Do what the dice tell you to. But with magic."

That sounded deceptively simple.

Fen took the dice and handed them to me. "You first."

"Who's my target?"

Dahlia winced. "You could use different phrasing?"

"Whomever you want," Fen said.

Alrighty then. We should get on with this. I rolled the dice, and they landed with the words *blow toes*.

I raised an eyebrow. "Not very erotic." This was Fen's idea, including making me choose where to start. Conveniently enough, he preferred to roam the house barefoot. "Foot out. Hurry it up now." I made a *come here* gesture.

He unfolded his legs and extended one in my direction. With another wave of my fingers, I stirred the air and let a light breeze brush his toes.

This was ludicrous. "Does that excite you?" I asked flatly.

One corner of his mouth pulled up. "It's foreplay. If I came with the first touch, that wouldn't be very fun, would it?"

I couldn't argue that.

"Who goes next?" Dahlia asked. "The rules don't say."

Fen grabbed the dice. "I say the person who got blown gets the next turn." His roll produced *bite fingers*.

"That sounds dangerous." Dahlia looked as skeptical as I felt.

"If sex is done right, it's frequently dangerous." Fen grabbed her wrist as he shifted enough for his teeth to elongate into sharp canines. He drew one of her fingers into his mouth and nipped.

Dahlia yelped, but with the second playful bite, her surprise melted into a sigh of pleasure.

Damn it, was I already enjoying this?

Thunder crashed outside the window, and Dahlia jumped. As the entire night sky flashed brighter than daylight for half a blink, she laughed. "Scared me."

"Best way to overcome that is to see what the dice want you to do." Fen picked them up and handed them to her.

Magic crackled in the air, from the building storm outside. Not a threatening kind of magic, but the type that was impossible to ignore.

When Dahlia took her turn, the dice landed on *Kiss* and *Nipples*.

Not subtle, but far more in line with what I expected.

Dahlia pushed her clothed breasts up, toward her face. "Do you think they mean mine or someone else's?" There was no hesitation in the action. No indication that this was meant to be seductive or playful or that she was embarrassed by the behavior. It was so very Dahlia.

And *that* was sexy. Was my mood lifting?

"I'm certain we decided your target is up to you," Fen said.

Dahlia scrunched her face up, as if in thought. "Nipple kissing, but magical. Okay." She rolled onto her hands and knees. The way she crawled toward me, ass in the air with a playful sway, was exactly the same move she used on stage. It was sexy and I liked it.

She lifted her hand mid-crawl, never pausing, and my shirt vanished.

Neat trick. "You don't want to use that mouth on Fen?" Not that I minded being her target.

"Frequently, but you'll enjoy this more."

I won't. The words flittered away the instant I thought them. I still felt anger, but now it was more of a memory than an emotion. I did have more sensitive nipples than Fen.

Dahlia climbed up my body, paused at my chest, and flicked a playful pink tongue over each sensitive nub. It was as fun to watch as to experience, and it was only two licks. Her playful smirk when she backed up said she knew how teasingly brief the moment had been, and she held my gaze until she was seated again.

This time when the thunder boomed outside, it carried a light feeling, sliding under my skin in the best way possible. I grabbed the dice and rolled.

I lost track of the dice, and sank into the game.

Licking Fen's lips while we floated in mid-air. Kissing Dahlia's toes. Laughing when she made Fen turn his ears into wolf ears, just so she could blow on them. His whimper flowed into a howl and he tackled her.

Dahlia was giggling while Fen growled, and I couldn't stop smiling at the energy in the air. The two of them rolling around together. My joy wasn't simply at the lust, it was that all three of us were the source. This was potent and compelling and *real*.

More thunder shook the building, but at this point it was part of the fun.

A soul-shattering scream ripped through the room.

"Magnus." Dahlia was on her feet in an instant, sprinting toward the door.

What were we about to find? It didn't matter. Fen and I raced after Dahlia, and into Magnus's apartment.

We found her in her bedroom, her auburn wings extended and her full Valkyrie armor in place, with a glazed-over look in her eyes. We were in trouble.

"Magnus." Dahlia grabbed her arm and shook her gently.

Magnus let out another roar, this one more primal, like a battle cry. "I'll destroy you for this." Her threat rattled the walls.

Fuck. "Hold her," I said to Fen. "Don't let go, no

matter what." I couldn't ask Dahlia to do that. She'd cave if she thought anyone was hurting Magnus, even in the act of helping.

Fen grabbed Magnus's arms and pulled them behind her back. She screeched and struggled. Her blade appeared in her hand, already held in the right direction, and stabbed through Fen's leg.

He howled in pain, but didn't let go. "Do this now." He spoke through gritted teeth.

Already working on it. I stepped up to Magnus and cradled her face in my hands. Or rather, gripped as tightly as I could without crushing bone.

She didn't give me a choice.

The emotion hit me like a truck, slamming into my chest and nearly knocking me away. So much desire, laced with grief, betrayal, and enough loss to clog my lungs.

I felt it all, and pushed back. I followed each thread to Magnus's core, the passion that made her who she was, and I muted it all. The glowing embers that gave me my power, that I dined on without thought from the world around me, faded into dull embers as I extinguished them. As I worked, her struggling diminished, and her screams quieted.

Why did I have to do this? Why did I have to mute who I was for others to go on? My anger grew. Swelling. Turning into white-hot rage and then the kind of fury that nearly blinded me.

When she slumped to the floor, nothing existed for me but the drive to destroy it all. I needed the world to burn, to make this feeling stop.

CHAPTER 14

FENRIR

"Frey." I kept my voice quiet, but firm.

He stood a few feet away, fists clenched and frame slumped, as if he'd fallen asleep on his feet, but angry. The only movement he made was the shudder of his shoulders when he dragged in a deep breath, then let it out.

"Get. Out." His words were low. Threatening.

Dahlia was kneeling next to Magnus, cradling her, and looking between her and Frey. She opened her mouth.

"Don't." Frey snapped off the word.

I had a good idea what was going on, and needed to diffuse without anyone here. Even Dahlia. I stepped between her and him. "Take Magnus and go," I said to her. "Somewhere safe. I'll find you later."

For a heartbeat, it looked like Dahlia was going to argue. *Please don't let her argue.* Instead, she gave a curt nod, and she and Magnus vanished from the room.

"That immature, irresponsible—"

I cut Frey off with a kiss, crushing my mouth to his and letting all of my desire, eons of needing him, flow through the connection. I broke away long enough to growl, "Don't say anything now you'll regret later."

He stared at me with a narrow-eyed glare, and when he opened his mouth again, I claimed it again. Biting his lips, tangling my tongue with his, and pushing him until his back hit the nearest wall.

I'd had my suspicions earlier, about where this anger was coming from. The dice game and his shift in mood showed me there was something to the idea, and what was happening here, after helping Magnus, all-but confirmed I was right.

If he was yanking her from the nightmare by muting her passions, Frey may be doing the same thing to himself in the process. And a god who was required to deny who they were at their core was a dangerous thing. He was smothering his literal reason for existing.

I intended to give him a jump-start. It was easy to let my love flow. Regardless of what happened, whether I was fighting someone else, with him, or we were doing something simple like working or reading in the same room together, the desire was always there. I *always* needed him.

Frey shifted the balance of power in the kiss, pushing into me, making us vanish from Magnus's and appear in our own living room. He shoved me into the couch with enough force that something cracked.

Good.

He straddled my legs and kissed me with the kind of force that would bruise a mortal's lips. The touch was all-consuming in its sensation, but it was only physical. The connection that usually bound me to Frey was twisted. Wilted.

I rolled both of us to pin Frey beneath me, and the couch creaked in protest. I didn't try to hold back my need for destruction, but I let my love for Frey blend with it and flow through everywhere my mouth touched, while I ripped at his clothes.

He reached for me, and I pinned his hands to his sides with a warning growl. I wanted to devour the man I lived for. "Let me worship you tonight."

Frey worked his jaw, but no protest came out. He didn't struggle as much under my touch.

I dragged my mouth down his body in a series of hungry bites, ripped off the remainder of his clothes, and took his cock in my mouth. The way he knotted his fingers in my hair and held me captive was enticing in a way I wasn't used to. I was in control, but not.

As promised, I worshiped him. His cock. I licked and stroked and fondled, knowing each of his cues. Knowing how much he was enjoying this.

And when his hips bucked and he fucked my face with swelling intensity, I felt that love flowing between us. Passion personified. The bond that connected us tugged at my heart.

Frey spilled down my throat when he came, and I devoured every drop before moving up his body to claim his mouth.

He spun me away into the couch, and I caught myself on my hands. This creak from the furniture was louder, and the entire thing gave underneath us, sending us on a short but jarring trip to the ground.

The tension seemed to break along with the couch, and we both found ourselves laughing loudly, leaning against each other for support. His touch against my skin was delicious seduction, rather than angry desperation.

We adjusted our positions, so I could slide into him from behind. The merge was soothing and electrifying at the same time. I didn't hold back as I fucked him hard and fast, holding him against me and memorizing every touch and sound. The salt of sweat on his skin when I licked him and the sight of him wrapped in joy.

When I came I felt it through my entire body—

not just the physical, but the emotional. The magical.

We collapsed next to the former sofa, wrapped around each other and using one of the arms to lean against.

"I don't know where the rage comes from," Frey muttered. "But it's all-consuming."

I leaned my head against his. "I do know."

"Don't keep me in suspense." Frey's laugh was strained, but he sounded so much more like himself.

I explained what I'd observed, about him suppressing himself to help the people Minato had trapped.

"Well, fuck." He sighed and more of his weight rested against me.

"You have to promise me you won't do that again," I said. "We'll find another way."

"I promise to save it as a last resort. Not doing it may not be an option."

"It has to be." Was this what it had been like, watching me for centuries, wondering if I was going to turn feral again and give into the wolf inside?

The circumstances weren't the same, but I was terrified of losing him to anger, and this was something I couldn't fight. Sure, I could fuck the fury away, but how long until that wasn't possible?

There was another concern, too. One I wasn't ready to voice to him. Each time this happened, Frey turned on Dahlia, and if I had to choose between them...

I couldn't. I wouldn't. I'd never betray Frey; in a million years he'd still be mine.

But I couldn't surrender Dahlia either.

The only other option was to make sure we didn't reach a point where that became an issue.

CHAPTER 15

DAHLIA

I always liked visiting Kirby, Brit, and the others. Sure, Magnus and I jokingly called them The Rescue Rangers, because they spent a lot of time tracking down and helping people with the potential to become immortals, but they were also a lot of fun to hang out with.

It sucked that so many times when I dropped by, bad things were happening.

Magnus was waking up when I landed us on the front porch of Gwydion's home in Wales. The house was in the countryside—a large, three-hundred-year-old manor surrounded by trees and acres of lush green.

"What a fucked-up dream. What are you...?" Magnus straightened from the position I had her in, with one of her arms over my shoulders, and me holding her up. "Why are we here?"

"Minato." I wasn't sure if that would explain everything, but I suspected it might.

She frowned. "On me?"

I nodded. "And Frey helped, but then—"

The door latch clicked, and I stopped talking. I didn't have a problem telling our friends what was going on with Minato and Vidar, but it felt like a betrayal to mention that Frey might be losing his shit, and we didn't know why.

Besides, he wasn't going nuts, he was just a bit pissed off because his realm had been destroyed and was being continuously invaded. I got that. I'd been furious when the first TOM campus was leveled, and I didn't even like it there. But it had been the only place I'd known as a home.

"It's about time you came to visit." Kirby grinned when she saw us. "I was starting to think you'd made up the part about Magnus being alive still."

I huffed. "As if. Here she is, in person and brilliant."

"Hiya." Magnus waved.

When I thought she was dead, it had fallen on me to let our friends—mostly Kirby and Brit—know. But that also meant I got to share the news when I found out Magnus was alive.

Kirby stepped aside and opened the door wider. "If you're here for game night, Starkad says he's never doing that again, and Gwydion says he wants to be a paladin this time."

"A paladin is lawful good and swears fealty to a single god. Does he know that?" I asked.

Magnus huffed a laugh. "My guess is *yes*."

"What's wrong?" Kirby led us through the front hallway, and toward the main sitting room.

Why would anything be wrong? Why would you assume we're not really here to game? Because we'd dropped in unannounced. Magnus was wobbling on her feet. We rarely visited anyway.

Kirby didn't have to be a master of reading body language to know things weren't right.

"We were attacked. NEON was destroyed. There's a vindictive twat out there who's working for Vidar who can give people waking nightmares. We don't know how to stop her. She came after Magnus." *Frey is mad. So very mad. I don't know why.* "NEON was destroyed, and it's horrible, and I don't know what to do and I'm not sure any of us does, but we left because..." *Frey is losing his shit.*

I trailed off in a sigh when I realized Kirby and Magnus were staring at me, and Brit had joined us and was doing the same. "I'm good, how are you?" I smiled weakly.

"More curious than you can possibly imagine." Kirby jerked her head toward the sitting room. "We'll ask questions, you give us answers, and The Rescue Rangers are on the job." She winked.

That made me feel a little better. So did this part of the house. There was a sofa and a few chairs, but mostly a corner of the room was covered with pillows and other large cushions on the floor. It was like a pit of comfiness, that made it easy for all four of us to sit near each other.

It'd be fun to do something like this in our house.

Fen and Frey's house. The correction popped into my head without permission. And Frey had lost his patience with me.

„."Where are the others?" Magnus's question drew me from my thoughts.

Thank the gods for not having to live in my own insecurities right now.

We all settled in, the casual setting a sharp contradiction to the fact that we were about to discuss destruction on a mass scale.

"Improv convention in Reno," Brit said with a straight face.

My laugh slipped out, and Magnus joined me, but we stopped when we saw the other two. "You're serious?" I refused to believe it.

Kirby nodded. "Gwydion loves the improv."

"And the others?" There was no way...

"Min says no one fucks more than people who met online and decide to get together at conventions, and Starkad..." Brit trailed off with a smirk.

The way Kirby laugh-sighed was a unique experience. "He likes the shows too."

Magnus and I exchanged glances. Super weird, but not the strangest thing we'd seen with this group. And they made fun of us for liking D&D? Whatever.

"Okay, give us real answers," Kirby said. "Start with the *vindictive cunt working for Vidar.*"

"Twat," Brit corrected her. "She definitely said *twat.*"

Magnus sighed. "Does it matter?"

We all knew better than that. Kirby raised one eyebrow. "Details always matter. Don't leave anything out, even if you think we already know it."

For the next several hours, we went through everything that had happened, frequently several times, with Kirby and Brit asking questions meant to draw out nuance, and Magnus and I answering as best we could.

We weren't getting anywhere, and I was so tired of telling this story, but at least here it felt like we all understood each other. If I asked, I was almost certain all of us would sign on to go find Minato right now. To take this fight to her door.

But I still didn't know where she was. I had a computer program supposedly based on my ability to find anyone anywhere in the world, magic plus tech and I should've been the perfect setup. But it had never pinged once with information about Minato.

Made me wonder why Vidar was hunting me for creating it. Why he was trying to destroy Magnus for helping me enhance it.

"Wait, back up." Brit sounded abruptly excited. "There's a fairytale involved."

Oh. *Oh.* Brit had been obsessed with fairytales and about true love overcoming evil magic for years. Since she found out most of them were based on real events, no matter how loosely.

I nodded. "About a bride and a husband and an evil witch."

"You're going to have to be more specific," Brit said dryly.

Fair enough. I related the story Frey and Fen had told us, and as I laid it out, Brit started searching on her phone.

"I do know this one." She was talking to herself as much as to us.

Kirby looked surprised. "You couldn't have mentioned this when they first ran into Minato?" There was no malice in her question.

"The story is about an evil witch, not a dream-devouring psycho bitch." Brit didn't pause in whatever she was typing on her screen.

"To be fair, Frey and Fen said the same thing." I was willing to overlook the past omissions as long as we got answers now.

Brit jabbed her phone harder with each passing second, until she growled with frustration. "I can't find it."

"Find...?" Magnus asked what the rest of us were thinking.

Brit sighed. "When I read it, years ago, I thought there was a hidden meaning behind the connection between the bride and the husband. I was hoping"—another sigh—"I wanted it to be a story about finding a loved one beyond the grave and bringing them back."

Because she'd thought for years that Kirby was dead, and that Brit was to blame. Another reason she wouldn't have associated the story with Minato.

"So I spent a lot of time tracking down the origins of the tale," Brit continued. "And at one point, I had almost pinpointed where the tale had taken place. It was in the US, eons ago. Before any recorded history."

That didn't make sense. "It's a European fairy tale. And if no one wrote it down, how do we know it?"

"Good question." Brit scrubbed her face and set down her phone. "But I can't find the information I did back then. I didn't save my research, because it didn't lead anywhere."

Research was Magnus's and my specialty. "Let's find it again."

The four of us gathered computers and moved into the library. Gwydion had so many ancient books. It wasn't quite like Artura's place, but it was still incredible.

I heard from Fen that Frey was better. That they needed to spend a few days healing, and as long as I was safe, I should stay here. He also explained that what was going on wasn't my fault.

Except that it was, because Minato was after me and what she was doing was causing this in Frey.

It hurt that Fen didn't want me with them, but I also understood. Especially when Fen ended the conversation with *I love you. I'll come for you soon. Always. I promise.*

The simple words warmed my heart and soothed my soul, but they didn't make anything else better.

CHAPTER 16
FREYR

I hated losing control. This feeling of my own self slipping through my fingers. Fen's theory about why I was dealing with abrupt bursts of anger made sense, however, I wasn't sure that mattered. I wouldn't hesitate to act again. To save Magnus. To save the people in the bar. To save Fen or Dahlia.

I hoped I didn't have to break my promise to Fen.

For now, fresh energy flowed through me. I was energized and rested.

Something's missing.

Nothing was missing. Except perhaps for replacement furniture. However, unlike NEON, the furnishings here didn't hold a deep emotional attachment.

To a lot of people, that wouldn't make sense, but Fen and I had broken more than one couch coffee table over the years, and I'd learned where the important pieces should go.

In addition, NEON was *actual* home. The bedroom was. The clearings where Fen went to spar and escape city life. The living room was simply a space where we welcomed guests and existed in-between life's moments.

It didn't take me long to make a call to Grendel—not his real name, because I couldn't reproduce the sounds that he made in his native tongue. He was a kobold who was always willing to take the old, broken items in exchange for new.

Within no time, the living room was back in order.

Dahlia would be disappointed she missed the fun.

Fen pressed his chest into my back and wrapped his arms around my waist.

Something's missing.

No.

"How are you feeling?" Fen asked.

"Good." Speaking the words aloud made them more real and helped me grasp that I was doing better. We did have a solution. "Better than in a few days."

Fen nuzzled the back of my neck. "Good."

In fact, I had energy rushing through me that was impossible to ignore, and it attached itself to an idea. A memory. "Do you remember when I put the first wards up, binding NEON to the apartment?"

"I do." The growl that rumbled from Fen's chest and through my back was delicious. "We invited all our most deviant friends. We were the center of attention."

He'd fucked me in front of all of them, at the orgy of the decade. I'd drawn on the desire that night to bind both buildings to me. To make this all mine. Ours.

I didn't need to have the orgy again, because the building was still part of me. Both of them were, even with the wards gone. Disappointing, but our world wasn't in a great place to have the connection back in place and neither was NEON. However, the purity of what I had with Fen currently flowed freshly renewed through my veins. "I can restore the wards now. Come to the club with me."

"Of course." Fen slipped his hand into mine, and I blinked us to the other side of the world.

Landing in the middle of the dining room should have filled me with warm familiarity. Instead, seeing the emptiness left me cold, as it had every time I'd been here since Minato invaded. The sensation sat like a series of heavy stones weighing me down.

The passion from the sex still flowed through me though. It was electric and potent and with Fen here, it wouldn't fade.

"What do you need from me?" He asked.

"Be here. That's it for now." I stood in the exact middle of the structure and closed my eyes.

It didn't take much focus to find Fen's passion. The ferocity he had for life, for battle, for me, and for Dahlia. The ethereal glow was vibrant and red, dancing in the air like chaos, and touching the edges of my own. Mingling and merging with it.

Someone's missing.

No.

This was the beginning of the same technique I used with those Minato had touched, but the steps diverged quickly. This time, instead of smothering Fen's passion and my own, I breathed gentle gusts into them, like stoking the embers of a flame.

He let out a sound that was half-groan, half-growl. Guttural and primal.

It was delicious.

I fed the *flames* until they roared around us, encompassing us and the entire room in a wash of my power. I pushed it out further.

The brightness flickered and protested.

No.

I paused and pulled back enough to restore stability to the magic. Once it roared again, I pushed out.

Once again, it flickered and pulsed.

This wasn't enough. If I pushed harder, to try to encompass both buildings, the passion would stretch too thin and snap.

"What's wrong?" Fen's voice was soft, but full of concern.

I didn't know. This should be working. My eyes flew open. "Fuck me. Here. *Now.*" The words came out with more desperation than I intended.

Fen pressed into me without hesitation and crushed his mouth to mine. The strength in his fingers, as he gripped the back of my neck, seared me to my core.

This was what I needed. I kissed him back with everything I had. I tugged us both together and wrapped our own love around us, until none of the outside world could penetrate.

Ice pierced my thoughts. Lonely. Cold. Angry.

The magical flames everywhere around us flickered and died. *Poof,* gone without a trace.

Was I broken? What good was a god of passion who couldn't *feel* passion?

CHAPTER 17

DAHLIA

"How did you know the information you found back then was related to the original fairytale?" I asked Brit. A better question might be *why did you believe...* But there was power in the way words were used, and I didn't want to go into this telling her we didn't believe her.

Brit didn't look bothered by the question as-is. "TOM had a lot of old books."

"Which we don't have access to now," Magnus pointed out.

The way Brit smirked said it wasn't an issue. "I've been using the dark web. Turns out it's good for more than just porn that'll make your blood curdle, guns, and drugs. Though some of those guns..." She made a kissing sound, popping her fingers away from her lips.

That was kind of brilliant—not the gun thing,

but using the deep web to find actual copies of old books. I'd forgotten, but I was the one who showed Brit a few years ago how to do exactly that. Because someone, somewhere was digitizing ancient tomes, if one knew where to find them.

We set ourselves up in the war room Gwydion had installed in the house for Kirby and Starkad. The place was brilliant. A large, heavy table in the middle of the room about two and a half meters long and one meter wide. It wasn't enough to stop an enraged berserker—Starkad, I assumed—from flipping it, but doing so would take enough effort to make him pause.

The walls were covered with white boards and cork boards, and the chairs were comfortable as fuck.

We picked our seats and hopped online. Min owned large stakes in many technology companies, since people watching internet porn fed his faith reservoirs the way NEON clients fed Frey's. That meant we had one of the best connections in the world, and under almost any other circumstance, I would've been in heaven.

This entire situation made me too somber to enjoy the best high speed internet money could buy.

The research rabbit hole ran deep. Alice wouldn't have comprehended how far we fell. But several hours of sifting revealed an issue—there was no way to tell what was real and what wasn't.

"We'll make some lists." I grabbed a dry erase marker, picked a board, and wrote out lists of elements we were finding in each story. The bride wielded a knife in one tale, a scythe in another, and a long, folded blade in a third. The witch's tie back to the real world was either a crown of thorns, or a rigged ring, or a bed of nails.

We tried to cross reference all of it. When did it all appear together? Apart. How many times did each element show up?

The only thing any of the stories had in common was that element of *true love*.

"That's because true love saves you in any fairy-tale where love is the moral," Brit said as it was the most obvious thing in the world.

At Magnus's frown, I changed the subject quickly, and moved us on to the next book.

Many hours later, the last several days—combined with sitting in a stuffy room and making zero progress—weighed heavily on me, and Magnus didn't look like she was doing any better.

We decided to call it a night, and Kirby showed us each to guest rooms.

Magnus looked beaten down by more than just a long day, so I opted to join her in the same space, rather than taking my own.

The rooms were decorated like they were straight out of a movie. Four-poster beds with canopies, beautiful wooden furniture... Except the pieces in here weren't intricately carved and detailed. They looked more like their original trees, but they radiated a kind of love and respect for their native shape.

Gwydion drew his power from the plants and trees, from the land, and it made sense that he'd offer their corpses respect in his home.

"I'm fine." Magnus told me when I walked into her temporary room. "Long day. I'm just exhausted"

But it was more than that. She'd been going hard, and we hadn't talked at all about what happened to *her*. "Nico," I said.

Even with her back to me, the shudder that ran through her body was obvious, and the quiet sob that punctuated it was heartrending. "What about him?" Her voice was clear, but she didn't face me.

"That's what I want to know. Talk to me. Tell me if it's the encounter with him weighing on you. Tell me without everyone watching and without having Fen following you and without stupid accusations, what's on your mind?"

When Magnus turned, agony and frustration splashed across her face. "Of course what happened with Nico is weighing on me. And with Bragi, and all of it. I'm fucking tired of trauma moments. And that we treat them like they're status quo—because they are—and that we have to just keep going, every single day. I should be there, with him. Or at least have plans to meet up. I was going to go back and remind him who I was. Or *something*."

But then the gods happened. Again. "You should go. Now." I meant it. If helping Nico remember would also help Magnus heal, I wanted her there.

Selfishly I also wanted her here, but this was about her.

"What would I *actually* do there?" Magnus asked "Let him tell me again that I'm pretty but forgettable? Let my personal needs take me away from this thing that's critical? That impacts so much more than me personally? We need to find Minato, and not just because she made each of us think the other was dead. I can't walk away from that before it's done. She's going to keep coming after us. She's going to make Vidar double unstoppable."

"Okay." I sat on the edge of the bed and pulled her next to me.

She sprang to her feet again in an instant, bristling, and paced. "Don't. Don't be reasonable, Gods damn it. Don't be nice about this. Be angry with me, or on my behalf, or *something*. Be Dahlia— the woman who gets pissed and excited and passionate about everything. Do that for me."

"I *am* angry." Speaking the words made them real. Made the feeling *real*. A dam broke inside me, and my frustration surged out. "I'm fucking furious. How dare Nico forget you? After being lovable and sweet and healing you. How *dare* he not remember how amazing you are? And Bragi lied to you, under the pretext of protecting you. He locked you away. He kept us apart. If I ever see his smug face again, I'll punch it. With my dragon claws." I scowled at how dumb the words sounded in the middle of a rant.

Magnus shook her head and huff-laughed. "I think that's called cutting, not punching. But Bragi, he..." She shuddered again. "He pulled me back from death. He healed me. He made me fall in love." Her voice cracked. "He let me think I'd lost you forever."

"And you're trying to hate him with all your heart, but some of what made you fall is still there." I wasn't dumb enough to think she could flip a switch and any affection she had for Bragi would vanish.

She sank to her knees in the middle of the rug. "I hate that part of myself, and I don't know how to scrub him out of my heart. And Nico... I barely knew him, but he seemed to actually care, and now... And... And..." She wilted.

"And what?" I hated seeing her this way. I didn't know how to do anything. *Just be there* seemed like such bullshit advice when my best friend was falling apart in front of me.

"And you have your entire life still." Magnus seemed to choke on the words. "Yeah, Frey's having a few bad days, but Fen adores you as much as he does Frey. They'd both do anything for you. That apartment is yours. I'm just a guest. You had them while I was gone. You had everything."

I didn't have her, and it hurt to hear her resentment. I understood it, though. "I know."

This time her strangled laugh ended in a sob. "Fuck you."

Anything I could say felt pitiful compared to what she was going to, so I joined her on the floor, wrapped my arms around her in a tight hug, and kept my mouth shut.

AFTER A NIGHT of restless sleep and a breakfast that I wished I could enjoy because Gwydion's cook was incredible, Magnus and I gathered in the war room with Kirby and Brit again.

"Okay. I'll write, y'all throw words at me." Magnus took a spot at a fresh board, marker in hand. Her pain was tucked away masterfully, the way we'd been taught, but I saw it in the way she tapped her claw-ring on her leg, and in the shift in tone. *Y'all* wasn't a word she used unless the region called for it.

I understood why she was tucking it all away. Some pain was private, and she had a job to do, the way we all did. "First story on the docket this morning claims the bride wielded an electric knife." I would help, if Magnus wanted to dive into work.

"Ahem." Kirby didn't sound amused.

The look Magnus shot me said she wasn't either.

"An electric knife. So that's obviously *not* from the original tomes."

"But it's part of one of the stories out there, and we need it all, to figure out some sort of pattern," Brit said.

I painted smugness into place and pointed at her. "See?"

"Fine." Despite Magnus's huff, she wrote *electric knife* on the board. "You know those things aren't even made for stabbing or slashing. Who cuts flesh with distinct serrations?"

"Eww." I pushed out my disgust, as if we weren't all thinking the same thing Magnus just said.

Thanks, training. *Not.*

As the day wore on, we gorged ourselves on soda, chips, cookies, and pizza. One of the best things about being immortal, that no one ever talked about, was we didn't have to stick to a strict diet to maintain the TOM physique. After a lifetime of being denied junk food, we all tended to go nuts with it on occasion.

Day bled into night and crept into the next morning. Dawn peeked through the windows, illuminating wrappers and boxes on the table, and boards littered with words and lines and boxes.

I was feeling a little nauseated, and I didn't know if it was from the food or the lack of progress.

Brit read a passage aloud, and my stomach gurgled. A chill sped down my spine.

Was I sick or was that... "Read that again," I said.

Brit did. The words were a little different this time, but they held a similar meaning.

There was that icy sensation again, like someone dragging a magical ice cube down my back. No, it wasn't potent enough for that; this was more like a trickle of condensation. "Read it in the original language."

"Uh... Don't dock me points on my pronunciation." Brit fumbled with a few words—not as many as I would have—but she managed to read the whole passage.

And as she did, a tingle encased me, culminating in a tug at my core, like an invisible string was connected to the page she'd found. "That's it," I said. "That one is important."

"Are you sure?" Kirby didn't look convinced.

Magnus erased a large section of the board and wrote furiously. "If she says she's sure, she's sure."

My magic was connected to the digital world, but I tended to write off the link because nothing I'd done to access it on purpose had worked very well yet. Like the program I wrote that should've been able to locate Minato.

But this... I felt it. The bond was real. The texts Brit was currently looking at were ancient and powerful.

Neat trick. "Let's keep looking." Now that I knew what it felt like, I should be able to identify it better.

As we discovered each new book, I added it to a digital archive, for reference later. Within a few hours, we had a new list, that was much cleaner and more concise, and coordinates for where to look.

None of us were certain the latitude and longitude were correct, they couldn't be, but at the same time, my instinct screamed for us to investigate.

So I brought us there, and we found ourselves. standing in front of a cave in the middle of the Appalachian Mountains in Tennessee.

This wasn't where I expected to be looking for fairytale history.

Not that there was anything here. It really was just a cave that looked like it hadn't been touched for hundreds, maybe thousands of years.

"So that's that." Magnus sounded disappointed. "All that work for nothing."

We all plopped down on the ground, frustration flowing between us, and a somber silence settled over the group.

We didn't have any less information than we had a few days ago, but we'd pushed so hard, and to have it lead to nothing...

As we sat in silence, a chilly breeze whipped around us. I summoned enough fire magic to warm the air. The cold probably wouldn't kill any of us, but that didn't mean it was comfortable.

A tingle raced over my skin. Was that my magic?

No. It felt like me. Like the magic my dragon

summoned, but mixed with what I felt when Brit was reading from the book she found. It was like an aged version of the heat I had wrapping around us.

This wasn't a cave. "There's more here." I stood and wandered toward the empty black void stretching out inside the rock.

CHAPTER 18
DAHLIA

As I walked up to the cave entrance, I expected to become a real-life cartoon, and walk into a flat wall that was just painted to look like an opening. That was the feeling that radiated around me—something was here that I couldn't see.

But nothing stopped me. I kept moving until I was several meters in, and turned around and rejoined my friends.

"What's wrong?" Magnus asked.

How to describe it? "I can't shake the feeling that there's more here. Something similar to what Frey does with NEON..." What he used to do. Sadness settled into my core, and I tried to shake it away. "To what I did with our apartment. And it tastes like someone used the same recipe as me, but it wasn't me."

Weird analogy. The way Brit stared at me in confusion reinforced that.

"Someone you're related to." Kirby tapped the empty air. Was she feeling anything? Looking for something specific. "Vidar?"

No. I shook my head. "This is kinder. More sedate." Like fresh baked cookies cooling on a countertop, while happy voices echoed in the background.

If I squinted, would I see it?

I was barely aware of doing just that, because the action came naturally. I half-closed my eyes and let my magic reach for the barely-there strands wisping around us. The more I tugged, the more I was able to grasp. There *was* more here.

I didn't want to shatter the spell that kept this second layer hidden from view, but if I plucked the right string, I could tug an opening big enough for us to walk through. Reaching out, I took Magnus's hand. She took Brit's, who took Kirby's, and the four of us stepped forward.

And then we were standing on a stone path that led through trees and native grass, up to the entrance of a Victorian house. Or mansion, more like.

"Where are we?" Magnus extended a hand into the air, the moonlight glinting off the claw-shaped ring I'd made her. It gave her access to a bit of my power. "I can't feel anything. As in, there's no magic in the air."

But there was. It was everywhere. It was light, a barely-there feeling that was pervasive. The brush of glitter on bare skin. "I think this is supposed to be where the cave is, but it's not on Earth right now. It's a realm I haven't been in before."

Looking at the house, the place existed out of time. The yard was an immaculate garden. There was no cracked paint on the house. No warped boards or rotted wood. As we approached, the curtains were brightly colored rather than faded or yellowed with age.

"How old is this place?" Brit asked. "Two or three thousand years?"

"Not nearly old enough to be from the original fairytale. " Tension ran through Kirby's entire frame as we approached. Her body was coiled, ready to pounce at the slightest movement.

Magnus and Brit held themselves in a similar way.

It wasn't necessary. I could feel, this place was safe. "It's about a hundred fifty years old." How did I know that?

Victorian mansion.

Except I *knew* my estimate was right. As though I could pinpoint the exact date it was abandoned and hidden, if I needed to.

"How do you know that?" Brit asked.

"I just do?" Shitty answer. Not the kind of response any of us would accept. But this entire setting spoke to my soul.

Magnus studied me for a moment, then nodded. "Okay."

Gratitude flitted through me that she trusted me that way.

"But we don't think the *actual* original bride from the *actual* original event lived here," Kirby said. "The tale was created centuries ago."

"Everything we found pointed us here." As she talked, Brit cast her gaze around the front porch.

But we were all doing the same. For me it was a combination of the training that said I needed to be alert, and the fascination with why I thought I belonged here.

Kirby gestured without words, pointing each of us into a medium-sized, fanned out circle, close enough to come to each other's aid in a blink, but far enough apart that most surprise attacks would only catch one of us. She always fell into the lead naturally. "Everything pointed us to the cave location, not a house in the middle of nowhere. Literally."

"This might not be where the story happened, but there's something about this place. It's relevant." I *knew* it. I just wished I could say what *it* was or why I was so positive. Our human-square twisted as we neared the porch, and I stepped up to the door.

The others moved into defensive postures

behind me, with Kirby watching the rear and Magnus and Brit ready for whatever might come at us when we opened the house.

Nothing sinister waited for us inside. Nothing obvious, anyway. The decor matched the time period, and like outside, nothing had aged. There was no dust. No cracked or peeling wallpaper.

"Fan out. Secure the location. Keep your eyes peeled." Kirby spoke softly, but with authority.

I'd do this by the books, but the instant we proved it was safe here, I'd explore.

Why was I so confident that would be the outcome? The safe feeling inside warred with the knowledge that no new circumstance or location was without threat.

Was Minato manipulating this situation? It felt real.

But her dreams always did.

Magnus pressed her arm into mine. Her brow was furrowed. "What did Bragi say to me the first night I showed up at his house?" She asked quietly.

I shook my head. "I don't know. You never told me." Something I low-key worried about was that she'd given me the story, but refused to dive into some details.

Magnus gave me a tight smile. "You're right, I didn't." She broke off into her own direction.

The four of us regrouped a short while later to

report the house was clear. Creepily frozen in time, but clear.

"Spread out, look for anything that indicates where or when we are," Kirby said.

Magnus pursed her lips. "*Hey, gang, let's look for clues.* How Scooby Doo."

"You have a better idea?" Kirby looked amused rather than annoyed.

"No." Magnus gave a quick shrug. "I'm just saying."

Brit tapped her chin. "I always thought of us more like Nancy Drew and her friends."

Her math was a little off, and I hated to be the one to point it out, but I would anyway. "There are four of us. I assume you're Nancy Drew?"

Brit looked at me and then Magnus. "And the two of you are my friends."

That worked for me.

The huff Kirby gave was exaggerated. "That makes me what? The boyfriend?"

"I mean..." Brit left the unfinished thought hanging.

"Nope." Kirby popped on the *p* "Solely and completely because Nancy Drew wore the strap-on in that relationship."

"I mean..." The way Brit's smirk slid in was perfect.

Though we all laughed, it didn't alleviate the

tension in the room, and our amusement vanished in a blink.

"What are we looking for?" Magnus asked.

Same thing as before. "A locket. A tiara. A blade."

"Loki already gave you the dagger," Kirby said.

The way the three of us looked at her, the collective thought of *and you trust him* rang louder than any shout, though none of us said anything.

Kirby sighed. "Yeah. I realized how that sounded the instant I said it. Ran rout. Rook ror crews. Dibs on Scooby snacks."

I doubted any of us wanted any snacks we found here, but her bad impersonation made me smile.

I wandered down a long hall on the main floor, past a couple of large rooms meant for people to gather, and toward a door across from the kitchen. That same energy that tried to soothe me and make me believe I belonged here was strongest in this spot. Regardless of whether the feeling was a lie or real, I'd find answers in here.

It was an office. Bookcases lined the walls, and their contents seemed to sing my name. At the far end, near a curtain-covered window, was a large desk. Like everything else in the house, it looked polished and dust free, as if someone used it yesterday.

There wasn't much on the desk itself. An inkwell that shone with bright black ink when I opened it. The same magic protecting everything else had kept it fresh. A blotter, a wax seal, and a letter opener. When I brushed my fingertips over the handle of the latter, a zing sped through me.

Dragon's claw. The hilt was made of it. I lifted the blade and twirled it between my fingers, testing the heft. The weight. It almost felt like I'd made it, but not quite.

"Dahlia, everyone, I think you should see this." Kirby's shout carried into the room.

She didn't sound panicked or in danger, but a call like that required action, and I sprinted back toward the sound of her voice. She was in the middle of one of the rooms I'd passed. Rich furniture surrounded her, but she stood staring up at a painting over the mantle.

When I followed her gaze, I understood why she was transfixed. It was a family portrait—mom, dad, and daughter, who was probably about twelve.

I'd looked almost exactly like her at that age. The girl wore my face.

Fucking creepy.

"That's Lance." Magnus's comment came from behind.

Who? Right. Lance was the personage Skuld wore at the end of their life. A dragon could take any shape, and they chose to be male. To appear as the head of the Followers of Urd. I'd never had a chance to meet my dragon parent, so I couldn't have been expected to recognize the face, but I couldn't stop staring at mini-me.

"Is anyone here getting horror movie vibes off this place?" Brit asked. "Any moment now the walls will drip with blood, the portrait will move, and voices will tell us to *get out*?"

"A bit, yeah." Kirby finally looked at us.

Magnus nodded. "Totally."

"Then why do I feel safe here?" I was asking myself more than them. "It feels like... Home."

"Of course it does. You're the kid in the picture." Brit pointed above the mantle. "Is this where you lived before TOM?"

We'd all been orphaned. It was why TOM was able to pluck us from the system. But unlike the others, I'd learned since that my parents were Vidar and Skuld. "It's not me..." I traced a thumb over the letter opener I still held. "It might be my... hundred and fifty year old sister? Shame I'll never meet her." None of the dragon children had become anything more than mortal until me. Artura drove that point home with me again and again.

I brushed my fingertips over the backbone of a nearby sofa, and the images in front of my eyes shifted. My friends were still here, but they were overlaid with transparent visions of the people in the painting. The scene had the same sensation as a dragon vision, but I was looking at the past.

Mom and Dad sat in their respective chairs,

reading and doing needlepoint, and mini-not-me was stretched out on the same piece of furniture I touched now. She had a canvas in front of her, and was drawing or writing something.

It was like I'd been dropped into the middle of a real life Disney Haunted Castle.

"Dahlia." At Magnus's insistent tone, the past vanished and the only thing left was now.

I shook my head to rattle away the images, but they stayed imprinted on my mind. "I saw the past. Nothing bad. Just the family, spending the evening together." Most. Banal. Vision. Ever. And I was here for it.

"We've all figured out this was Skuld's house and that's why Dahlia feels connected to it, right?" Brit asked.

Magnus wandered through the room hovering her fingers over various surfaces, but not making contact with any of them. "Not in so many words, but..."

"It makes sense," I agreed.

The look Kirby gave all of us said she thought we'd gone loopy. "How does it make sense?"

"How does a Valkyrie being reincarnated thirteen times, and having the same name and appearance in every single life, make sense?" I countered with an *explain that* look of my own.

"Point made," Kirby said. "But you can't just assume anything."

Brit raised her hand and wiggled her fingers. "I still don't understand what this place has to do with the fairytale."

"I think you want to see what's in the upstairs bedrooms." The way Magnus spoke, she thought her suggestion would hold all the answers.

"Our best and our brightest, or our only real survivors, and none of you have learned anything." Vidar's voice came from behind us, and I jumped. "Why did fate choose any of you?"

My blood turned to ice, and my instinct screamed at me to *run*.

No. We were fighting. My claws extended, and Magnus and Kirby were instantly in full Valkyrie regalia, charging him. Brit didn't have a nifty transformation, but she did have a loaded Jericho 941 that she appendix carried, and it was already in her hand.

In a blink, Kirby and Brit disappeared. Where the fuck did they go? Magnus struck empty air when she reached Vidar. He'd already vanished and reappeared elsewhere in the room.

"I've been looking for this place forever, and you walked right in without so much as a pause." He kept speaking as if he wasn't under direct attack.

If he'd been looking for the home, the last thing he'd want to do was risk hurting it. I was willing to take that chance, for a chance at him. I charged his position, but expected him to blink out of sight. The instant he vanished, I did the same, reappearing in the part of the room with the fewest obstacles.

Vidar was near the mantle instead. "No time to play catch today. Sorry, kiddo." Sarcasm bled from his taunt. "The house was Skuld's. The story is about them."

"Bullshit." I struggled to balance rage—the need to destroy him—with the knowledge I needed to be smart about this. Magnus appeared behind him while his attention was on me, but he was already gone again.

The scene fuzzed out of focus, then swam back into view like a slightly out of sync, double exposure.

Please, not now. I couldn't do a vision now.

But it was worse than that. Everything was happening now, as I saw about three seconds from now overlap it all.

Vidar was already in the doorway when he appeared. Talk about confusing. "I don't care if you believe me, and I will have to come back later to play. Tonight my only goal is to destroy that locket." He snapped.

But the house had already gone up in flames in my vision, and I watched it seconds before it happened in real life, with no time to stop it.

The only thing I could do was assume my dragon form and wrap myself around Magnus. I wouldn't lose her again.

Heat roared around us, searing but not burning,

as Magnus's magical shield overlapped mine and we kept each other safe. The flames were gone in less than a minute, and so was the entire house. We sat in the middle of a pile of melted steel and brick, with ashes snowing down around us.

Whatever the house had been, my legacy or just a distraction, it was gone now, and an empty pit sat in my chest, aching for a place I'd never really known.

How were we supposed to fight Vidar? No matter what we did, he was always one step ahead of us.

FREYR

The last few days of spending time with Fen had me back to center, but it felt like something was missing. The house was down a person, and I noticed. It had me on edge to not have Dahlia here.

When my phone rang, I was surprised to see Kirby's name on the screen. I expected Dahlia on the other end when I answered. "Hello?"

"Are Dahlia and Magnus there?" Kirby barked the question.

Like that, three days of peace vanished under concern. *Where is she? We need to find her.* "She's supposed to be with you."

Fen's attention shifted from casual interest to high alert at my statement, and I put the phone on speaker.

"She was with us," Kirby said. "We were

following a lead, but Vidar showed up, and then Brit and I were back home. *Poof.*"

Not everyone had the ability to phase from one place to another, and neither Kirby nor Brit could. But Vidar was perfectly capable of sending them away.

My concern soared. I reached my magic out, let tendrils float across the world, searching for that signature I knew was Dahlia's, or at least Magnus's. "I don't feel them anywhere."

"I don't think we were in this realm," Brit said.

That complicated things.

And then I felt Dahlia. Outside the front door. The lock slid open, and she walked in with Magnus.

"She's here. Just now," Fen said.

"Intact?" Brit's question had me concerned all over again.

Dahlia crossed the room in a blink. "Is that Kirby and Brit?"

"What happened?" Kirby asked.

This was about to get chaotic. "That's what I'd like to know."

Magnus scowled. "Fucker destroyed it all."

"Destroyed what?" I assumed we were talking about Vidar, but the rest was a large cloud of nothing.

"Nothing left?" That was Brit again.

Dahlia's huff did nothing to match my growing frustration. "That's what *all* means."

No sense of decorum with these four when they got together. No sense of order. So why was I watching Dahlia with affection instead of frustration? "Some of us are missing details about this conversation."

"Right." Dahlia met my gaze and the apologetic smile she gave me was sincere and sweet. "We're safe, we'll call you back," she said into the phone, then reached over and hung up.

Fen cupped her face between his hands and pressed his mouth to hers in a kiss I felt in the depths of my soul. It was one of those sights that soothed, but a thread of something I didn't recognize ran through my reaction.

The feeling vanished when they broke apart, and I kissed her on the cheek. "I'm glad you're both safe."

Magnus was fiddling with something that looked like a neat stack of old pages. not paper, but possibly sheepskin.

"What is that?" I nodded at the *book*. "What happened? Kirby said you ran into Vidar. Start at the beginning, not at the part about Vidar." I added the last bit as Dahlia opened her mouth.

She frowned and paused.

"We found an old house of Skuld's," Magnus said.

"Supposedly," Dahlia added.

Magnus sank into her chair with a huff. "There was a portrait with them in it, and a little girl that looked just like Dahlia. And she knew how to find the place in the middle of the mountains in Buttfuck Tennessee."

"That does sound telling." I sat next to Fen, and he tried to pull Dahlia down to join us.

She chose to pace instead. "Even if it was, I'll never get to explore. Vidar destroyed it all."

"I believe we covered that part." I felt sorrow on her behalf. To find those links to her heritage, and have them snatched away so abruptly, must be hard. But I was glad for her that she'd gotten to see hints of who Skuld was before.

Dahlia tugged on a strand of hair. "We thought the house might hold a link to the fairytale. When Vidar got there, he said he'd been looking for the place for a long time, and that if he destroyed it and all its contents, the locket would be gone too."

"Which sounds like total bullshit." Magnus was half talking to us, half looking at the book she'd brought home with her.

"What is that?" Dahlia nodded at it.

Magnus held it up delicately. "It's what I discovered when everything happened. It's probably the last thing left of the house. You should have it."

Dahlia gave a quick shake of her head. "No. Because Vidar was lying, and that means it's not mine. You found it; you should keep it. If it was true, why wouldn't Artura tell me? She said she'd been researching what Minato was, not *a Baku fought*

Skuld once and this fairytale was taken directly from their life."

"Because no immortal has ever kept the truth from us, and Vidar is the only liar we know." Sarcasm oozed from Magnus's voice.

Dahlia looked around, brow furrowed. "What is that?"

The air had shifted in the room, adding a new magical presence that felt like it was growing.

"What did you do, you incorrigible child?" Artura's booming question landed as she appeared in the middle of our living room.

No walking up to the front door and knocking. No greeting us like a polite ancient being. Simply intrusion and demands. It was infuriating in its lack of decorum, and even more so because this building simply was. There were no wards stating this place was not hers.

Not that it would have kept *her* out.

"You'll have to be more specific." Dahlia stared Artura down, defiance in her voice.

Though Artura looked on the surface like a petite young woman without a care in the world, her smile held eons of knowledge, and sent a chill racing up my spine. "Skuld's home," she said. "The last remaining reminder of who they truly were. Before corruption. Before devastation stole them and left us with you."

Artura's derision, her scorn, clawed over me, and

Fen's low growl told me he felt the same. I didn't mind letting him have a turn, but his reaction would be more violent, and the room wasn't currently in any condition for a dragon to fight a wolf.

I stepped forward before he could act. "You will not force your way into our home, and hurl insults."

"No?" Artura turned on me. "Are you certain you want me to leave? This is the part of the story where your hero demands answers, and I can't give them to her if I'm not here."

"We'll find them oursel—"

"Is it true?" Magnus talked over me. "What Vidar said?"

"Not you." Artura bit off the words. She snapped her fingers and Magnus stopped talking, though her mouth was still moving.

Dahlia stalked forward, practically radiating fury. "Don't touch her. Don't talk to her that way."

"She's not the *hero* of the story." Artura sneered.

"She's my sister. She's my family. This is *not* a *story*," Dahlia said *story* with mocking, "This is our fucking lives."

Artura chuckled. "This *is* a story. One I've seen play out half a dozen times. And if Vidar is the reason the house is gone, you've lost the locket, which means your quest, your story, is over."

Then it was true. Vidar had told them at least a little of the truth.

"You could've told me." Though she spoke to

Artura, Dahlia was focused on Magnus. Kneeling next to her. Pressing a hand to her throat. Magic flowed between them, but still no sound came out when Magnus worked her jaw. Dahlia glared at Artura over her shoulder. "I came to you for answers, and you *lied*."

"I tried to tell you the truth." Artura's smugness was infuriating.

I worked as subtly as I could to draw power into me. I grasped the furious passion, the righteous anger and desire to protect, from Fen, Dahlia, Magnus. From anywhere I could find it outside the building.

Dahlia told Magnus softly, "We'll fix this," and turned to stalk toward Artura. Purple flame flickered around Dahlia like an aura.

Artura looked unimpressed.

"You did lie," Dahlia said. "You told me you'd been doing research. Implied the story was unfamiliar to you. But if that house was Skuld's, if the locket was the key, you watched them live it, didn't you? You know exactly what Minato is capable of, and that Skuld dealt with something similar once upon a time."

"Do you really believe that after thousands of years on this planet, having become sentient before sentience existed here, that you're the first person who's wanted my advice?" The power rolled through Artura's voice.

Tension coiled through me. How much had been kept from Dahlia? From all of us? I tugged harder, drawing more power into me. There was no need to look at Fen, to confirm he was ready for this. He was ready.

"I'm the first new dragon though." Dahlia's confidence flickered, but roared back in a surge of visible magic.

Artura barked a laugh. "No. If you survive, that will be a first."

My power flared with my anger, wrapping around Fen, Dahlia, Magnus, and I, not to take us away, but to protect us.

Fen's features shifted as he let part of the wolf out.

Artura turned her gaze on us. "Calm yourself, *gods*." She spat the words.

I didn't intend to fight unless we had to, but it was rapidly becoming that type of situation. "There have been other dragons. Is that what you're implying?"

"That's what I'm *saying*," Artura said.

"What about all those things you said, about not being able to teach me to control my power. About—"

"All true." Artura cut Dahlia off. "I can't. I've never been able to teach one of you, and neither has Urd. You're stubborn and willful."

One of Dahlia's most endearing traits, despite the frustration it sometimes caused.

"That's not a bad thing." Fen growled.

"It's gotten them all killed, and it makes you impossible to teach." As Artura spoke, her presence seemed to grow, despite her size remaining the same. "If you don't learn on your own, for some reason the information is less valuable. So I nudge. I poke. And I scream silently as you make mistakes I have answers to, because if I told you outright, you'd discount the truth."

Unbelievable. This being who had asked for trust, who had promised assistance and answers, had decided there was no reason to actually give either one.

"I would've listened," Dahlia said.

Artura sighed. "But you didn't."

"Because you were never telling her the truth. Why would she be expected to hear more lies, when her entire life has been filled with manipulations?" I was furious on Dahlia's behalf. "Who are you to dictate what she should and shouldn't know?"

"*I* am the person with the answers," Artura said.

No. This was insulting. "Will you give them to her now?"

"No."

"You hold yourself above all others." As I spoke, I grew my presence to counter Artura's. "You believe you're somehow the ultimate in authority. That you can do no wrong. And yet, you are as petty, as manipulative, as narrow-minded as every being you look down on for the same.

"*Get out.*" My roar echoed, and Dahlia's shout mingled with it. I felt her power overlap and mingle with mine, colliding with Artura's, then pushing it back. Pushing *her* back.

And then Artura was gone from the apartment. I wasn't certain if it was by her hand or ours, but she was no longer welcome in my realm.

"I need to replace the wards. I need to do it now." While this power still coursed through me.

"I'll help. But I need to fix Magnus, first." Dahlia knelt in front of Magnus again and placed her hands gently on Magnus's throat.

As far as any of us knew, dragons couldn't heal others—though it was possible that was something Artura kept to herself as well—but if Dahlia could break a *curse*...

A soft purple glow radiated around the spots where the two women connected. The light flared brightly for a moment, then vanished.

"Fucking cunt is *still* manipulating us," Magnus shouted.

CHAPTER 20

FENRIR

I wasn't surprised to discover Artura had kept secrets from Dahlia. Had lied to her. When it came to beings who had lived many lifetimes, it seemed the older they got, the more convoluted their logic and plans got. I'd rarely met an immortal over five-hundred who knew the meaning of *keep it simple, stupid*. And once they passed two-thousand-years-old that number dropped significantly.

That didn't stop me from being furious about the situation.

Magnus's exclamation wasn't surprising either, but then she grabbed the book she'd brought back. "What does hngfynth mean?" she seemed to be asking herself as much as any of us, and she flipped through the pages with delicate reverence.

"Bless you?" Dahlia said.

Magnus turned the book so we could see it, but

kept it close to her. "I recognize most of these words, or can figure them out in context, but not that one."

The bottom fell out of my thoughts as I stared at the drawing and text. It was eerily familiar, because it was a drawing of a single moment, in the scene that had just played out in our living room. And it was written on a medium that hadn't been widely used in centuries, in a language that hadn't been spoken for nearly a thousand years.

That supposedly had never been written.

I suspected the only reason Magnus could read it was she'd been taught by gods who used to speak it.

"What the fuck?" Dahlia's question matched my thoughts.

It was like an ancient version of a comic. The artwork was intricate and beautiful. The images were stylized, but there was little question it was us. Dahlia, Frey, Magnus, me, and Artura in the middle of it all. Power clashing with power as Frey and Artura faced off in a battle of wills.

"I'd just started looking at it when Vidar showed up." Magnus turned to earlier pages as she spoke. "I didn't recognize that scene, but this one..." Her voice went soft. The picture was her with Nico. Him telling her he didn't remember her.

I could see how much she was hurting. She tried to hide it, and I wasn't the person to ask her to expose her pain. From everything I understood, the last month or so had been a lot harder on Magnus than it had on Dahlia.

"It's not everything, but it's a lot of what we've done since Dahlia and I found each other again," Magnus said.

Dahlia reached for the book, but pulled out without making contact. "Did Skuld draw that? Did her daughter?"

I had another question. One I hesitated to ask. "Does it say what we do next?"

"I haven't had time to look." Magnus closed the book. "And I'm not sure I dare."

This time when Dahlia reached out, she gently closed the book, took it from Magnus, and set it on the coffee table. "Don't look. There's no reason. If the cheerleader dies and we have to rent a Nissan Versa to save her, at least let us arrive at that conclusion alone."

"What *are* you talking about?" Frey stared at her, confused.

"Heroes. TV Show. Keep up." Magnus turned to Dahlia. "You know tales are frequently based on truth, even modern screenplays."

If she was suggesting that some obscure television program held elements of magical reality... It wouldn't be the first time.

Dahlia shook her head. "We're not letting some ancient cunty dragon tell us what to do next. You may think I'm being stubborn, the way Artura does, but the instant we start following someone else's script... We don't know how much of it is real. If they took any artistic license. If things have changed since then."

Magnus picked up the book again and flipped through it. "What if Vidar has something similar? What if this is how he keeps beating us to the punch?"

"We don't have answers." I would point this out if no one else would. "We're running out of time, and ignoring the book, going against it, is letting it dictate our lives as much as doing what it tells us to."

"Which is why we don't look," Dahlia said. "We figure things out on our own."

While I understood the point she was trying to make, she was leaving out a key element. "We look for answers when we don't have them. If that book has answers..."

Magnus showed us the page she was on. It showed Dahlia talking to a woman who looked vaguely familiar, in a place I swore I'd seen before, but I couldn't place either.

"That's the bakery in Australia," Magnus said. "Where Dahlia kept ending up when she couldn't control her powers."

And now an ancient comic book of questionable origins wanted us to go back there.

It was difficult to say which felt like a bigger mistake—staying or going.

CHAPTER 21
DAHLIA

Anxiety assaulted me at the idea of going back to Australia, enough that I asked Frey to take us there rather than doing it myself. The feeling grew when we appeared on the sidewalk outside a cozy little bakery, which was a shame because the place itself, the owner, had never been anything but kind to me.

But this was where my dragon had brought me before I learned to teleport. Twice. It was where TOM found me, and if I hadn't already discovered my immortality, it would've been where they killed me. I'd been hunted every time I'd been here.

Did Tania know who I was back then? She'd approached both times and offered the simplest, but also the sweetest help. Food. To use her phone. Rather than something like giving me the secrets to my heritage or fighting gods by my side.

As Fen pushed into the bakery, tension coiled inside me.

No one was here but Tania. No customers. No other staff. She stood behind a long counter with bar stools running along it. A TV was above her head, pointed at the small dining room consisting of a couple of tables, and about eight chairs.

She smiled when she saw us—a bright, genuine look that held no threat. "You're back." Her voice was kind. "Are you staying longer this time? At least some of you?"

That was an odd way to phrase things. I couldn't help but examine her every movement. Her words, her tone and inflection. It all looked normal. Had she known what I was the first time she met me? What did she know now?

"What can I help you with?" Tania asked. "Food? Drink? Something else?"

"All of the above, I'm hoping," I said.

Did Tania's posture just shift to something more rigid? Her back was straighter. Her smile looked frozen in place.

I didn't want to have to fight her—this woman who'd helped me simply because I was here.

But she wasn't mortal. I felt it where I couldn't the last few times we were here. She was old. Ancient. Primal magic whispered from her that had been around longer than Fen or Frey.

"What are you?" My question fell out before I could consider the words.

Magnus lightly smacked my arm, and I swore I heard Fen snort. If he hadn't, his wolf's amusement was still there, teasing my dragon.

"I'm sorry about that," Frey said. "What she means is, we're looking for a family heirloom."

There was no question, Tania looked different now. Stiffer. Filled with anticipation. "I'm not sure you and I are of the same family."

Weird, *weird* response. Fuck it—if she had answers, direct questions were the best way. "I'm Skuld's daughter. A very long time ago they took something from a witch—a Baku. They used it to save their husband. It might be a tiara or a diadem? Do you know where it is?"

Tania's chuckle caught me off-guard. "Gods, I thought you were never going to ask. I can tell you where to find what you're looking for, but it's my understanding that the task isn't easy. Before I can do that though, you need to prove to me you are who you claim."

Odd request since she seemed to already be certain, but okay. I held out my hand, palm up, and let it shift into a dragon's. My fingers became long, gnarled, and scaled, and claws extended from the tips.

Tania didn't look impressed. "A lot of creatures can change their appearance."

"*A lot* is an exaggeration." Frey kept his tone cool and practical.

A nice bit of balance, because I felt how on edge Magnus and Fen were. They were both ready for a fight.

"More than one can do it, and that means it's not proof," Tania said.

I didn't know how better to show her who I was. Multiple beings had the gift of seeing the future in visions, too. Besides, the whole *I'm going to tell you when and how you die* thing was so cliche, and not something I had control over seeing. A lot of beings could also summon wings. And fire.

But no one else could...

The thought flitted out of my grasp, but I snatched it back. Familiar threads called to me from where they snaked around Tania. I felt them wrapping her up. Binding and hiding her, like I'd felt when we found Skuld's house.

No. This wasn't quite the same. It was tainted with a darker intention.

Tania was trapped? Cursed?

I focused on the spell and reached for her, but didn't make contact. Now that I was looking for them, the ropes of the magic were distinct. At first they reminded me of my dragon magic, but the threads that tightened them looked more like...

Vidar?

The bindings were bright impressions in my

mind. I sliced at them with magic, and the bonds fell away from Tania.

Her laugh was one of relief. Bright and loud, and she abruptly looked thirty years younger. Odd thing for an ancient being, but I suspected this was her true face. "Oh my gods, thank you." Her voice cracked. "I never thought... I hoped, even though I shouldn't have dared."

"This was a curse, I assume." Magnus didn't sound so emotional. "Beyond that, what's going on?"

"Skuld trapped her. Or Vidar. Or..." I didn't know why or how, but I'd just sliced through the bonds. "I don't think anyone else could've broken the spell, like what happened at the house. But why?"

Tania was staring at her hands, turning them over and back, as if she'd never seen them before. "I was supposed to wait for you. I wronged them. Fought against them. This was my punishment. To keep the bracer—it's not a crown of any sort—safe until their worthy heir came along."

"Dahlia's been here twice before." Fen sounded as unimpressed, as unmoved, as Magnus.

Tania finally looked at us again. "And I so hoped she would be the one. I'm sorry, darl. I wanted to tell you, both times. I wanted to give you the entire story. Part of the curse was that I couldn't talk about this unless you asked direct questions, and even then I couldn't say much while I was trapped. I'm sorry."

Fear clung to her words. Another victim of the immortals.

I understood exactly where she was coming from. "It's all good, I promise."

"But I was told you'd be in today. He had a book that said... The curse. The promise... And when you didn't show, I was worried."

At that, ice filled my veins, and my good will faltered. Was she talking about the same comic Magnus had? Something similar? Everywhere I went, those fucking prophecies were dictating my life, even when I didn't know it. I wanted to ask her for all the information, but with so many lies, how would I know what was real? "Tell us where the bracer is."

"Sit. I'll bring you food and explain." Tania had vanished into the back before I could protest.

What else could we do? We made ourselves comfortable around the table.

"We don't trust her, do we?" Magnus's voice was quiet.

I wanted to. She radiated kindness and honesty, even now. Even though she'd kept things from me. But I was concerned about one thing. "She's following something *he said* from *the book*, and it's telling her the future? That never bodes well for us."

"It's possible we're walking into another situation like TOM and FU," Frey said.

Two organizations that spent hundreds of years—and were still doing it as far as I knew—hunting and either saving or killing potential gods, depending on what the dragons' prophecies said.

"We're here because we're out of options." The weight of Fen's words landed heavily between us. "Does anyone have any suggestions about where we would go instead?" As he spoke, he flexed his fingers. He was ready for a fight, and he was certain one was coming.

"Okay everyone, dig in." Tania was back, setting a large plate of sausage rolls between us all, and four pints of beer.

There was no way she carried all of that with two hands, without dropping or spilling anything, but my short term memory and a lovely tune flitting in my mind said that was exactly what she'd done.

"We'll eat, if you'll talk," Frey said.

The food smelled incredible, better than pizza or take out, and my memory said it was. But he had a point.

Tania nodded. "That's fair. Please, dig in."

We did, and she pulled up another chair, to sit a few feet back, between Frey and me.

"As I said before, you're looking for a bracer. Dahlia is the only one of you who can wear it. It takes a toll on its bearer, consumes their blood and their life, but a very small number of creatures can survive. Dragons. Baku. One or two other things that no longer exist. To touch it is to know excruciating agony. Crippling pain."

Lovely. I was looking forward to that. The idea made my food curdle in my gut, and I set my half-eaten roll aside.

"The bracer is in a similar place to the house you found, locked behind a ward only Dahlia can break. But she can't do it without Frey," Tania said.

That was disturbingly specific.

"That's a lot more detail, and a lot less riddle, than we're used to." Magnus's words reflected my concerns.

I glanced back at Tania to see her nod. "It is," she said. "Those are the instructions I was told to give you. The rest isn't so helpful."

Oh goodie.

She reached into her apron pocket, and I tensed. My concern didn't fade when she extracted a folded cloth napkin. She held it up in one hand, and pulled it open with the other, displaying a fishhook.

What the actual fuck?

She presented it to Frey. "I'm told you specifically can use that to find the right location."

I wasn't sure that was a good idea. As he reached for it, I asked, "How does it—"

The bakery vanished, and Frey and I stood at the

edge of a lake. Cattails grew a few feet away, and water crept up the edges of my boots.

"—work?" my question landed amid silence. That wasn't right. There should be crickets or frogs or some sort of noise from nature.

But there was no sound. Only a light chill and oppressive darkness.

"I suspect we're about to get more answers than we're ready for." Frey reached for my hand.

CHAPTER 22

FENRIR

"Where did they go?" The only thing keeping me human was the need to interrogate this woman. I bared my teeth and let my growl roll through the room.

Tania shook her head, and took a step back from Magnus and me. "I don't know. I did what I was told."

"Which was what?" Magnus asked.

"To give Frey the fishhook, and it would take them to the bracer. That's all I know. That and once they find it, they'll be back here." She looked panicked. Sounded it. But a confidence hid underneath, that floated on—

The thought vanished before I could grasp it.

This was all sorts of too wrong for my comfort. "What if they don't find it? What kind of trap did they just walk into? *Where are they?*"

"Or does your curse guarantee they'll find what they're looking for?" Sarcasm bled from Magnus's question.

Tania's back was to the wall, and her eyes were wide. "I don't know. It doesn't say. All I know is you're supposed to wait, and they're supposed to come back. If you hurt me, the beacon that brings them home will vanish."

That last bit didn't line up with *I don't know*. I growled louder, and let my jaw and nose become more snout-like, baring fanged teeth.

"What are you?" Magnus didn't sound any less angry than me, but she was better at speaking through the desire to kill.

"I'm a siren."

What? I nearly lunged for her throat. They were the daughters of one of the muses, and far more dangerous and deceitful in real life than in the legends. "Bring them back, now. Or you're the main course to that appetizer."

Tania looked at me with defiance, and the fear she radiated wilted, until I could see through the mask to the smugness below. "You don't understand separating from your clan, *wolf*? You of all people should know that family crumbles for reasons that are out of the control of the outcast. You'd call me one of them because we share a name?"

"I knew this was too easy." Magnus let out a barking laugh. "But we all walked right into it anyway. Dahlia's family cursed yours, and in return, the moment you were free, we thought you'd just make us lunch and give us answers?"

A medium-length blade—about the length of her forearm—appeared in Magnus's hand, and the anger she radiated was potent. "You know that a Valkyrie can heal, don't you?" The threat that ran through her words filled the air.

"Not other magical beings." Tania looked between us.

Magnus's smile was wicked as she took a step back. "You'd better hope that's not true in every case, because if it is, he'll be done with you too quickly."

She wanted me to torture Tania so Magnus could put her back together and we could start again. If Frey or Dahlia was hurt, I'd do it, but I was worried that Magnus went there first. I also wouldn't argue the point with her in front of someone else.

"I sent them to one of my sisters." The air around Tania seemed to shatter, and she took on an almost bird-like appearance. "I know that Dahlia isn't her family. That she broke my curse, and that she'll destroy her aunts. That's all I want. My sisters on the other hand..." Her beak-like mouth twisted into a too-human smirk.

I lunged, and Tania vanished. "You kill me, you torture me, they won't find their way home." Her voice floated on a tune that was more in my head than my ears.

I didn't believe her, but I'd have to find her to kill her. I looked at Magnus. "Draw her out and you can have your pound of flesh."

"You don't say." Magnus's smile was haunting. When light hit her blade, it seemed to vanish into the black metal rather than bouncing off.

Given the situation, I was here for it. The biggest problem was that this bakery wasn't big, and given the way Tania vanished, it wasn't as though we'd find her hiding behind the counter.

But we'd figure it out, and then there would be hell to pay.

CHAPTER 23

FREYR

Where were we? As I reached out my senses, there was no indication of an outside world. It was as if we existed in a void, and by the feel of things it was less than one-hundred acres, and was mostly lake and shore.

I couldn't even tell if we were in another plane, or on earth but cut off from it, the way NEON had been.

It didn't feel safe, regardless.

"This place has a major creepy-crawly vibe. Or is that just me?" Dahlia rubbed her arms, but didn't erase the visible goosebumps running along her skin.

I shook my head. "It's not just you."

A light touch whispered over me. A charge. The pull of seduction wrapped itself around me, making

my pulse race and my desire climb. I could do something similar to this, but this was warped. Deceptive.

Effective. It tugged at my thoughts, sifting out
the need to touch. To seduce. To control.

"What is that?" Fear tinged Dahlia's voice.

"Lust." It tugged at my core and my cock. If I
weren't on edge, it would draw me in and wrap
me up.

The sound Dalia made was half-grunt, half-
whimper. "This isn't lust. This is..." She shuddered,
looking like she might be ill.

Was she feeling something different than I did,
or reacting to the same thing in a different way?

A light tune danced and swayed in my ears. It
was soft, sweet, and potent. *Be you.* The whisper was
a sensation rather than words, carried on a beauti-
ful-but tuneless folk song, sung by a potent baritone
and a delicate soprano.

This was wrong. Whatever this was, it didn't
want good things from us. "We need to figure out
what we're doing here. Pick a direction."

"Why me?" Dahlia asked.

Make her.

What in the gods' names? "Because I trust you."

"Okay." One corner of her mouth tugged up in a
way that was distinctly her. "This way." She pointed,
and we started walking.

The darkness moved with us, swallowing the

world behind us with each step, like an inky black fog. Dahlia stumbled, and I reached for her, to steady her. As I brushed the small of her back, where her T-shirt had tugged up enough to expose skin, need shocked me.

Take her.

That was disconcerting. At the same time, carried on the music, sung to the seductive tune, it was reasonable. A good idea.

Which bothered me more.

"Do you have your phone?" I asked.

"No. My bag is at Tania's." More strains of fear wove with Dahlia's reply.

Delicious, tantalizing fear.

I rolled my neck and forced the music aside.

"But I have this." Dahlia held up her hand, and flame flickered to life in front of us. She managed to shield it in a way I didn't understand, to keep the light projected forward without letting it blind us.

She'd learned so much control over the past few months. Was becoming so much more.

Break her.

I could do that. I knew which buttons to push. Dahlia wore her weaknesses like a flag when she trusted someone.

She trusted me. *Oh, fuck.* I squeezed my eyes shut and gave a quick shake of my head, to try to rattle out the foreign voice.

"Are you all right?" Dahlia studied me with concern.

"Fine. We need to do this, though."

Was she hearing a voice? The music? Her shoulders were drawn in, and her gaze flitted everywhere, as if she couldn't take in our surroundings fast enough for her own comfort. She radiated *vulnerable*.

No more sass. No more mouth. Make her yield.

No. I pushed the response back, to whatever that was. Dahlia was her defiance. She was her independence and her brilliance.

No one could or should take that from her.

The music seemed to fade, until I only heard traces. A note here and there. Dahlia and I continued to walk along the water's edge, passing grass and cattails and rocks.

"Does it seem like we're going in circles?" she asked.

"It seems like a circular lake." And we had no idea how big it was.

Dahlia nodded away from the water. "I think we should go that way. See what else is here."

No.

The voice was soft. A whisper. But the compulsion it brought nearly rooted me to the ground. As much of me wanted to stay the path as follow Dahlia. There was nothing here but water. Only blackness. Only her.

"That way it is." I forced my feet one in front of the other, and we moved in a new direction.

The lake seemed to curve, to follow us. It wasn't circular after all. New scenery lingered in the shadows, just at the edge of Dahlia's light, and that seemed like a good direction to head.

We walked for several minutes in silence. I suspected she was straining her ears like I was, though it was odd for Dahlia to not chatter to fill the void.

Why are you here? The question sang in my mind, echoing my own thoughts, but with a different lilt and meaning.

Was that the odd voice still? Of course not. I didn't hear voices. It was me. Asking a reasonable question.

Dahlia stumbled again, and her pained cry twisted like a knife in my heart. She dropped to her knees and the flame in her hand went out.

I was at her side instantly, offering her a hand up. "Are you all right?"

"Yeah. Fine." As she stood and put her weight on her foot, she grunted and fell again.

I caught her before she hit the ground. Twisted ankle? On an immortal being who could heal nearly instantly?

She's weak. She can't hide it forever.

She was stronger than almost anyone.

When she wants to be.

"Come on." I scooped her into my arms, and moved directly away from the water. My steps were tentative in the lack of light, but I picked my way along what felt like a mostly smooth path, and we found ourselves at a rock face that seemed to have dry ground.

I set Dahlia on her feet, and she stumbled again with a muted whimper.

Delicious.

"What's wrong?" I was genuinely concerned.

She leaned against the stone and rubbed her foot. "It still hurts. It's not healing. Why isn't it healing?"

Whiny. Stubborn. Didn't know her place.

Stop.

Was my own voice getting softer?

They were all my thoughts. I didn't hear voices.

You are though.

Ridiculous. "Sit. Let me look."

"Okay." Dahlia sank to the ground.

She was so exposed like this. Hurt. Vulnerable. Easy to shatter.

No.

The music grew around us, swelling toward climax. If there were words, this was where the story would turn toward hope in the midst of strife.

When Dahlia looked at me, fear was splashed across her face. "What's wrong?" Despite the strength in her question, her fear seeped through.

It would be so easy to take her. Her desire wrapped around me despite the pain, or maybe amplified because of it.

This isn't me.

It was, though. This was the me I'd forgotten centuries ago.

That I left behind on purpose.

That I was forced to abandon. I dragged a finger up her leg, inching higher.

Stop.

No.

I could make Dahlia ours. No more fighting. No more gods hunting us. She would know that she belonged to us, and no one else would touch her.

She belongs to no one.

Not true. She was mine. She was Fen's.

"Frey." Dahlia pressed her good foot to my chest, and her leg steeled. "What are you doing?" The fear was still there. The terror. Scared little girl, needed to be safe.

Another push and she'd make a joke. Pull away. Refuse to take this seriously and block out reality.

I'd break her of that.

No.

"Freyr." Dahlia's voice was sharper this time. She sprung to her feet. The ankle, not injured?

I didn't understand.

I didn't care.

Leave her alone.

That shouting was so distant in my mind. It wasn't me. It couldn't be. I stood as well, and pressed my hands on either side of her head. "You're childish." The words passed my lips without thought, while a tiny portion of me protested, and a roar smothered my own mind. "You're impulsive. Immature. Not worthy of this gift."

That's not me saying those things. Stop telling her these lies.

But wasn't it? They were the unspoken things I never dared vocalize. "You think Fen belongs to you and he doesn't. You are tolerated. Nothing more."

"No." Dahlia's protest was weak, like the one in the back of my mind, but then she met my gaze with a hard look. "I am far from perfect." As she spoke, strength wormed its way into her words. "But I am trying. I'm learning."

Yes.

"Fen is ours. Yours in a way he'll never be mine." She straightened. "Mine in a way that he'll never be yours." She twisted her hands and slid them under mine.

A shock raced through me and my mind splintered. Rage screamed for me to fracture everything Dahlia was. A voice that was *not* mine. And my own mind wanted to make this right. Loathed what I'd been about to do.

"And in a hundred years, in a thousand, in ten thousand years, I will still be here. *We* will." A fierce power rocked in my head as Dahlia spoke. "We. Are. Infinite." She spoke at the same volume, but her voice seemed to shake the world.

The music shattered. Tinkling glass falling around my thoughts, taking its influence as it evaporated. I fell to my knees as Dahlia did.

"Oh Gods." The reality of what I'd been about to do rushed in, and I nearly vomited. Whatever that influence was, there was enough of me that wanted it to be right... "I'm sorry."

"It's okay. Sometimes I think you're a cranky old asshole." Dahlia sounded like herself again. "I mean, the words hurt, but I get it."

Was she making a joke? Now?

Of course she was, because she was Dahlia, and I loved her for it.

"No." The voice came from everywhere at once, both angry as it echoed in my ears, and musical and sweet inside my head.

The woman who appeared in front of us was stunning. Handsome and androgynous, with strong but delicate features...

That didn't make sense.

"A single moment of self-awareness does not save you." She was speaking, but her lips didn't move, and the furious song was seductive in my mind in a way I couldn't shake off. "I've been imprisoned for centuries, so you can find yourself, dragon. You don't get to grasp enlightenment in a matter of minutes and then walk away." She flew directly at Dahlia.

No. I moved in a blink, placing myself between them, and putting up an invisible wall.

Move. The voice was in my head, and I was flung aside. My body slammed against a rock face, jarring me. Healing was instant, but my shock lingered. What was this?

"You say you respect her, but you don't trust her to use the gifts she—"

Dahlia vanished from her spot, and reappeared behind the woman. "Suck on this, bitch." As Dahlia fired an attack, the siren vanished, and the flame flew toward me.

I brushed it off with a scowl. We needed to be more careful.

I lost track of time as Dahlia and I tried to pin down the siren. But each time one of us did something the other managed to undo it. We were causing each other more grief than the siren, and both Dahlia and I were showing the wear. Our clothes were torn, and scorch marks lay along our skin.

I pinned the siren in place with invisible bonds, and Dahlia swooped in with an attack. But the force was enough to break my captive free.

This was exhausting. Unlike sex, I could *not* do this all day. Especially when I wasn't in sync with my partner.

Dahlia blocked an attack from striking both of us, and paused next to me. If a battle plan was forming in her head, I couldn't tell what it was. She and I weren't made to fight together. I wasn't made to fight, period.

"If I contain her, can you kill her?" I asked.

"I can hear everything you say." The siren's voice was both beautiful and terrifying and seemed to come from all around us. "I am my realm, and you will suffer for betraying the woman you love."

Dahlia raised her brows. "Love? You? Me?"

So very much that I didn't know how I'd ignored it for so long. However, "this is not the time. And yes. Can you do what I asked?" I didn't care if the siren heard us. I could pin her down if I could see her, and then Dahlia could do the rest.

"Yes." Dahlia ginned.

Fantastic. Now we simply had to locate the threat.

"Be right back." Dahlia vanished, I felt an odd tug in the air, and she reappeared a blink later, siren next to her.

I threw up an invisible box without asking how she'd done that. Details would come when this was over.

The siren howled with fury, and the magic I used to hold her was fractured. Before I could worry about rebuilding it, the structure filled with flame.

That was all Dahlia.

The screams were horrific, a scraping down the spine kind of noise, and then it was done.

Peace. Finally. The voice seemed to sing all around us. The darkness bled into light, and the lake was just a lake, in a clearing, near a cave. It was calm and serene now, and I could see the outside world once again.

"We did it." Dahlia didn't sound like she believed it. Her hair hung in messy strands around her face and her clothes were torn in so many places. She looked tired, but beautiful and strong.

I didn't dare touch her, though. "I do believe in you. No one is like you." *I do love you.* The words were stuck.

"Nope." She gave me a weak smile. "They're not."

The battle had been glorious, and Fen would be sorry he missed it, but what came before still haunted me. I felt like a barrier hung between Dahlia and me. How was I going to make this right?

A bracer lay on the ground where the woman had been. Had it been there the whole time, or did she drop it when we destroyed her.

I reached for it, and the pain when my fingers brushed the leather was like having my fingers ground to a pulp while they were still attached. Still I tried to grasp it. Pain was my punishment.

But it was too much, and I couldn't stop my scream of agony.

Dahlia grasped the bracer, taking it away with one hand, while she covered my fingers with her other. She held up the bracer, summoned her bag, and dropped the find inside. It seemed the agonizing magic didn't impact purses. "We should go."

As she said it, the lake vanished, and we were in Tania's bakery again, but she was nowhere to be seen. Fen stood in the middle of the room as a wolf, snarling at the air, and Magnus was next to him, her wings out and a wicked-looking blade in her hands.

"You're back." That was Tania's voice, in my head as well as out loud, the way we'd just experienced.

"She's a siren," Magnus said. "And she sent you to her sister for lunch."

A siren. That explained a lot. I'd never run into one before, but I was familiar with others' stories. "Her sister is dead."

"*What?*" Tania's furious roar filled the room.

Dahlia vanished from sight and when she reappeared, Tania was with her.

In a breath, I imprisoned Tania in a box, the way I had her sister.

Fen and Magnus looked ready to kill.

Dahlia stood in front of Tania, studying her, nothing but an invisible wall between them. "This is what's going to happen," Dahlia said. "You helped me. More than once. You've been more honest than most anyone else, except the people in this room.

That's not a high bar, but it's still something. My family cursed you, you tried to feed us to yours in return."

Dahlia took a step back. "We're going to walk away. You're going to let us. And we're all going to hope we never cross paths again. If we do..." She glanced at all of us. "None of them are as nice as me, and it's been a bad year." A pained expression crossed her face, and she looked at Tania. "What?"

"You heard me," Tania said. "And I agree. Our fates and paths no longer need to pass. My sister chose her path, and I chose mine."

"Yes." Dahlia took Magnus's and Frey's hands, and I did the same, and we were back in the apartment.

"What happened?" Fen asked.

I didn't want to put it into words. Not for everyone. I wanted to tell him, but I needed to process. I wasn't myself out there. At the same time, I swore none of that was someone else.

"We got the bracer." Dahlia was subdued as well. "I think it's like Thor's hammer, but painful."

I could correct her. Thor was nothing like she thought, and neither was his hammer. She meant the movie Thor, and was probably referencing something about being worthy. I hoped she never had to encounter the real Thor, because she would be gravely disappointed.

Or worse.

"So we're all set." Magnus didn't sound certain. "Except for the fact that we don't have the knife. Or the locket. Or a location for Minato."

"Yup." Dahlia wouldn't look at me.

This wouldn't do. I needed to make things right with her. If I could. I wasn't even sure I could make them right with myself.

CHAPTER 24

DAHLIA

Only true love saves you.

Tania said the same thing to me, whispered in my head, as Brit said the other day.

Then again, if Tania was a siren her words were meaningless.

"Where did you go?" Magnus's question was direct, and that made it difficult to brush off. "When Tania said she was a siren I had visions of sailors being seduced to their death…"

A shiver ran through me. We were gathered in the kitchen, and I was grateful because right now I wanted the comfort of coffee and to pretend that was what was going to keep me from sleeping.

Magnus gave a wilted smile. "But that's not true, is it? Nothing magical is like what we think."

"No, that one's pretty much true." Fen handed me the jar of beans without me asking.

For a few seconds, the noisy whir of the grinder filled the room, shoving aside thoughts of seductive songs and the screeches of burning an ancient being alive.

Frey scrubbed his face. "That explains the music."

"You heard music?" I supposed that noise could've been called music.

The way Frey frowned didn't sit well with me. Neither did the fact that he kept looking away from me. He kept his distance. The moment by the lake hung heavy in my head, but I didn't want it to make him treat me differently.

"You didn't hear music?" He asked.

How to put this? "Have you ever listened to really bad death metal, where the band thinks the point is to suck and the lead singer growls more than sings?"

"Really bad, or really good?" Fen's laugh was tight.

"I heard a berserker band like that once," Magnus added.

Fair point. "What I heard was like nails on a chalkboard. Screeching. A voice that sounded like mine but wasn't me, and was in my head."

Magnus's cheer faded, but it had been forced to begin with. "What did it say?"

I didn't want to remember, and putting it into

words would make me do that. I might tell Magnus later. Maybe. "It doesn't matter now."

Frey's expression darkened further, which I wouldn't have thought possible. We needed to talk about what happened, and I refused to let him steer clear of me because of it. Was I forgiving too easily?

No. I knew who he was, and I always had. Him. Fen. I wouldn't have come to them again and again for safety if I didn't trust them. Sex or not, I would've always come back to them.

Trusting this way, without question, got me in so much trouble at TOM. Not because I trusted the wrong people, but because Vidar and Hel insisted I trusted too much.

Though they also insisted I needed to trust them more.

"We need to talk," I said to Frey. "You and me."

He clenched his jaw, and it was impossible to miss that both Fen and Magnus raised their brows.

"We just got you back," Fen said. "And you want to leave again?"

"Not far. Please." I already felt a chasm growing between us, and I wouldn't let him shut me out or go back to treating me like a fragile doll, the way he had when I first met them. "At NEON." Why did I add that?

I wasn't sure, but it felt important.

Frey exchanged a look with Fen, who frowned, but nodded. "I'll meet you there," Frey said.

As in, teleport myself? I was fine with that, but it seemed an odd request. I gave a quick nod, and blinked from the room. When I appeared in the bar, Frey was several feet away, near the stage. It was dark in here, but not the same kind of dark as near the lake. This was safe. Welcoming.

Even without the wards, it felt like Frey.

"I'm sorry." Frey kept his distance from me, and his gaze cast down. "What happened there... The things I did."

"You didn't do anything." I wasn't stupid. I was fully aware of what could have happened. Of what was probably supposed to happen. But it didn't. And if his experience was anything like mine... "The voice I heard told me I was nothing." The words sliced through me to say, but expelling them was a relief. "I could've sworn it was my own thoughts, saying I was weak. Pathetic. Worthless. That I'd never be anything."

Frey finally looked at me. "That's not your voice. It's Vidar's. Hel's."

"It became mine. Great gift, huh? What did your voice say?"

"It actually came from me, and I've spent centuries trying to erase that part of myself."

That didn't sound right. "Tell me."

Leaning into the stage behind him, Frey crossed his arms. His expression and posture were such a loud defense, I didn't know if I could step inside even as I closed the distance between us.

"It told me I could break you." His voice went cold. "That I could crush your spirit and make you bow to only us."

Fuck me. The words sat heavy in my gut, and from anyone else but Frey or Fen, they'd put me on the defensive. But, "That's not you."

"Once upon a time, it was exactly me."

"Then. Not now." I was close enough that if I reached out, I would just brush his arm. I took those last few steps.

Frey looked like he wanted to bolt, but he stood his ground. "I squashed that side of me."

He seemed so set on being guilty.

I didn't want that. "By choice. No one made you become who you are now but you. I know because the other gods are still the kind of beings who believe they should be able to crush anyone. To break them and own them. Vidar is still that way, but you chose to be who you are now."

"Why the fuck do you do that?"

"Do what?" I didn't understand.

"Why do you have such an unwavering faith in me?"

Because you're you. Probably not the answer he wanted. "I just... do." I needed to work on that. "Maybe that's who you were back then, but now it's who you're ashamed of. The same way I hate what

Vidar and Hel made me, and that's why the siren fed on it. I'm not as far beyond it as you are, and that voice, that song, wanted to make me believe I was everything I strive every day to not become again."

That was convoluted. Back up. Try again, me. "There are some things we can't change about ourselves—like you can't help being a super sexy god and I can't help being the most fantastically dressed goth ever—but at least part of who we are is because we choose it."

Frey's shoulders relaxed and his arms dropped to his sides. The way he studied me changed. His brow was still furrowed, but there was a softness in his gaze now.

"What?" I asked.

"You're a lot smarter than people give you credit for. I've always adored that about you."

Heat flooded my face.

"But you were still terrified of me," he said.

I shook my head. "No. I was terrified, but not of you."

"Of what then?" Challenge filled his reply.

"Of creatures that can make us into people we're not. That can feed us dreams that aren't ours and can manipulate us until we question everything about who we are and where we are and the people we love. I'm terrified that they're out there, and we aren't prepared to face them."

The way Frey reached for me, then dropped his

hand, made my heart ache. I grasped his fingers before he could pull away again, and stepped in until my toes met his. He pulled one hand free to brush a touch over my cheek so lightly, it was more of a suggestion than a sensation.

"Will you help me?" he asked.

I had no idea what I could do that he couldn't accomplish on his own. "With what?"

"To put the wards back up on the bar, and tie it back to the apartment."

No. "I—"

"You can. You're in control of your power, you're learning who you are—you just said as much—and I haven't been able to do this alone."

I couldn't make it worse, could I?

Oh, fuck. Could I?

Probably not.

"If you believe in me, then you have to trust that I believe in you," Frey said.

I was pretty sure it didn't work that way, but I didn't have an argument. "Okay. But don't get mad if I fuck it up."

He pressed his lips softly to my cheek, where he'd touched seconds earlier. "I won't and you won't." He moved to the side, farther from me, but only a meter or so. "Follow my magic."

An instruction that wouldn't have made sense six months ago. Now I didn't hesitate to close my eyes and reach out. I saw it, cords of power weaving into a grid. Glowing and growing until it was a solid sheet. I pressed my own will into what Frey was doing, and warmth blanketed me.

The ethereal fabric grew, spreading across the club. Through rooms I couldn't see from here but were clear in my mind's eye because I'd been in them so many times. Because this was my home.

I had to reach deep to keep up with him, but I felt Frey's strain as well.

Something in my mind snapped, and the entire thing rolled in on itself like the blinds in a Tom and Jerry cartoon. My eyes flew open to see Frey's deep scowl had returned. "What happened?" I asked.

"It's still not working. I think… I think NEON may be gone."

CHAPTER 25
DAHLIA

I refused to accept that NEON would never again be the place I'd fallen in love with, and not just because of the resignation in Frey's voice.

"We're tired. We've been fighting for days, even if it hasn't been physical. I'm certain if our roles were reversed, you'd tell me I need rest and maybe a few good orgasms," I said.

"That does sound like me." Despite Frey's chuckle, a thread of hesitation lingered in his voice.

He was still dwelling on what happened by the lake. Not the fight, but before that. I knew the impotence would haunt me for a while, and he was likely the same, but I wanted to take the next step toward moving past some of it.

"That wasn't you." I would say it again and again

until he remembered the same. "And it stopped before things went too far."

Frey looked like he was ready to withdraw again. "Because of you, not because of me."

I grasped his fingertips lightly, both of his hands with mine, and held on. "You were fighting it."

"I had stopped fighting."

That suffocating fear was back. Not because of him, but for the reasons I'd already given. The lack of power we had when it came to the immortals we were facing. I didn't like this, and I wanted the distraction as much as he needed it. "Are you going to never fuck again?"

A visible shudder ran through Frey. "Perish at the thought."

If this were Fen, and he had pushed too hard in a fight and injured me, if he was refusing to spar with me again, I'd push him until he did. And I'd enjoy the fight.

I was doing the same now for Frey, and had zero issues with that. "This is me asking you for this. You're not coercing me or forcing me into anything." Stepping closer, I settled Frey's hands on my hips. "Let's go back to Fen, and make a better memory to end tonight."

Frey brushed his lips over mine. "I've always loved the way you think."

This time, he took us upstairs without hesitation. Magnus had gone home, and Fen was waiting for us.

"How did it go?" he asked.

I swore I could feel Frey's disappointment. I hated that. I also hated that NEON was gone. I hated this entire situation.

Fen frowned, probably at the lack of response and our somber expressions.

I wanted to shift away from the bleakness for the night. "Can we take a break from bad news?" I needed this distraction as much for me as for them. I was desperate to stop thinking about how bad things had gotten. About the lack of control any of us had right now. "The sexy kind of break?"

"One of my favorite kinds," Fen said.

Frey's scowl faded. "One reason I love you."

He'd said he loved me, too. When we fought the siren. Frey didn't say it directly, but he confirmed it when the siren said so. I wanted to talk to him about it, should have done so downstairs, but I also didn't know if this was the time. *Hey, I know our world is falling apart, but I really need you to tell me you love me. Now.*

I'd settle—enjoy might be a better word—for watching the way Frey and Fen were kissing, and basking in the heat that flowed between them.

Fen grabbed me and pulled me to them, tugging at my heart, and making me feel wanted. He pulled me into the mix and kissed me so hard I felt it in my toe rings.

Then there were hands everywhere. Mouths on mouths. On ears. On necks. I didn't know which of them I was kissing, or who was devouring me, but it felt incredible. Clothes fell away, and I was pretty sure some of that was magical.

My Docs coming off for instance, because there was no natural way those were kicked aside without me noticing or magic. But I wanted to lose myself in this moment, rather than think about anything.

When we were all naked, Frey used his entire frame to guide me back to the couch, and nudged me to sit. He knelt at my feet, spread my legs, and kissed along my inner thighs.

It was tantalizing and not nearly enough, but I was willing to wait for more. For a little while at least.

Fen joined me on the couch, and lowered his head to suck on one of my nipples, while he kneaded my other breast. The position left his cock within my arm's reach, and I couldn't help but stroke. The sounds of pleasure he made hummed against my skin, as he continued to taste me.

I reached my other hand down to knot in Frey's hair, and urged him higher, but Fen grabbed my wrist, stopping me.

Frey kissed higher regardless, gliding his tongue

over my slick skin and sending shudders of desire through me. He parted my folds with a fierce lick, and drove his tongue inside me.

Oh, fuck. Frey's skillful movements were heaven, and my touch fell away from Fen as Frey treated me like a delicious treat.

I leaned my head back and let the pleasure roll over me. When Frey pressed his thumb to my clit, I jerked with surprise and delight. He stroked and teased, tongue-fucking me into bliss, and I ground against his face and hand. I was floating on clouds when I came.

It felt so good to be between them. So safe.

Lies. I'm not safe.

I banished the errant thought and focused harder on losing myself in the sex.

Frey moved up my body to kiss Fen. To share my taste. And Frey moved to me, crushing his mouth to mine. Devouring my moans the way he had my pussy.

"I want to watch you suck off Fen," Frey murmured against my mouth.

Yummy. "Yes, sir." I rolled onto my knees so I could take Fen into my mouth.

I loved the sounds he made while I was sucking on him. The way he melted into my touch. I was both powerful and lost to them when we were like this, and it was incredible.

Frey nudged my opening from behind, and slipped in easily, making me gasp. Now I was being roasted on a spit, even more trapped, and it was glorious.

Frey didn't move much inside me, but his girth and length were enough to remind me he was there, along with the occasional twitch.

I measured my movements by the delicious sounds Fen made, from grunts to, "faster. Harder. *Fuck yes.*" When he thrust deeper into my throat, tears welled in my eyes, but I took his length hungrily and readily. And when that first salty spurt hit my tongue, I devoured his climax with enthusiasm.

Fen had barely pulled from my lips, when Frey began a hard, fast pounding inside me. He dug the fingers of one hand into my hip, hard enough to mark me, and moved the other to my clit.

Fen reached down to tease my breasts again, rolling my nipples between his fingers. The onslaught of attention was incredible. Easy to revel in. I was too busy enjoying the sensations to recognize climax sneaking up on me, until I was caught in its throes.

I fell into the feeling of bliss, and Frey's grunts and punctuated jerks told me he was coming as well. For that moment, as we were both at the peak of pleasure, the world stopped just for us.

I didn't want to come down from this high as he softened and fell out of me, but I was willing to move into the bedroom, to cuddle between them.

With the sex over, and stillness settling into the room, my mind was free to race back to the encounter with the siren. I was happy with the outcome, but the fear and doubt, that terror of knowing we weren't in control, lingered.

With Frey and Fen pressed in on me, both of them radiating strength as they drifted between drowsiness and sleep, I should be as safe as was possible.

But in the silence, punctuated only by their steady breathing, fear rushed back. Not for me, but for them. For Magnus. For anyone who might get caught in the trajectory of the gods and my fate.

"Go to sleep, Ducky." Fen's voice was drowsy. He nuzzled the back of my neck, and draped a heavy arm over me.

He didn't push away my creeping worry, but he seemed to draw in the exhaustion brought on by the last several days. My eyelids drifted shut without my permission, and my fractured thoughts yanked me into dreams mixed with dragon visions.

It was an odd sensation, being a third party point of view in my own sleep. Watching things play out and knowing they were part fear, part prophecy, and all unwelcome in my head.

Vidar knew we were coming. He knew it because

he had a copy of the comic Magnus did, as we'd predicted. I watched, both horrified and completely removed, as he plotted and planned for us to invade. He was ready for us to walk through his front door.

When a chime sounded from somewhere in the dream, no one looked up. Was I the only one who heard that? Was this the power of the omniscient narrator?

My eyes flew open to the dark bedroom. I was still snuggled up with Fen and Frey, and the beep was barely loud enough to hear when I was conscious. It was coming from my computer.

I scrambled out of bed as quickly and deftly as possible, trying not to wake them in my rush to shut off the sound before Fen heard it. I opened my laptop and my heart dropped into my feet.

My program had finally found Minato. It knew where she was, and I was the only one who knew that.

I could wield the bracer. We didn't have the knife or the locket, regardless of how many of us joined in this hunt. If I could get to her before she figured out I was on my way, I could end this now. The people I loved wouldn't have to suffer anymore.

Frey stirred, and I froze, not daring to even breathe. After a moment he settled in again, and his breathing evened out.

I dressed as quietly as I could, and stashed the

information about Minato for future reference, just in case.

I gave them one last look. "I love you both," I whispered in the darkness. And to Magnus, *I'll be back. I promise.*

I blinked out of the room, to scout Minato's location.

CHAPTER 26

FENRIR

I love you both.

The words echoed in my head. Something wasn't right. The air felt wrong. *Smelled* wrong.

My eyes flew open, my wolf sensing what was wrong before my brain caught up. "Dahlia's gone."

Frey was awake in an instant. "Are you certain?"

"Yes." Consciousness was becoming concern. Her scent was already fading. I climbed from the bed. Why did it wake me up? Why was I so worried? "She left her phone." As well as her bag, her computer, and a note on top of it all. "Went to destroy Minato. Back for dinner."

The flippant tone would be cute if it weren't for the content of the note. My growl rolled out long and low.

Frey didn't look happy either. A look of focus passed over him. "I can't feel her."

"*Fuck.*" *What are you doing, Ducky?* "Odd's she told Magnus?"

"More likely than most things." The fact that Frey was yanking on clothes indicated how serious this was.

I did the same, and within moments I was hammering on Magnus's door with the side of my fist.

She answered looking less than impressed. It didn't matter that she was wearing pajama bottoms and a camisole—she'd be a threat to most of the people who could wake her up.

"We're sorry to—"

"Dahlia is gone," I cut Frey off. Not the time for niceties.

Concern replaced Magnus's drowsily irritated expression. "Late night taco run? Does she do that?"

"Have you ever known her to do that by herself?" I handed her the note.

Now Magnus was scowling. "Stupid idiot," she muttered, then looked at Frey. "You can feel—"

"Already tried that." Why were we talking? Talking wasn't taking action.

Turning away, Magnus opened the door wider. "How do we find her?"

"We were hoping you'd have an idea," Frey said.

I didn't like this. Caged. Unable to act. My wolf whined and I paced in response.

Magnus vanished into her room and emerged less than a minute later, dressed and looking ready to throw down with the next person who pissed her off.

"She whispered before she left." *I love you both.* If she was hurt when we found her... I didn't know what I was going to do. "And I may have heard beeping before that, but I thought it was part of a dream."

Magnus perched on the edge of a chair, and grabbed her laptop from where it sat on the coffee table.

Act. Now.

We were. As much as I hated that this was what taking action meant.

"*Fuck.*" Magnus's gaze flicked back and forth across the screen. "Her program got a ping." Magnus had a copy of the same software Dahlia was using to look for Minato, because Magnus used it to help Kirby find Valkyrie locations, and because Magnus helped write it.

Something told me she wasn't talking now about having located a Valkyrie. "Where? Why are we still here? Let's go."

Magnus shook her head. "Dahlia locked me out. I can see that the alert came in, but she deleted it."

Despite the fact that Frey stood still, his frustration was palpable. "So it's gone?"

"That's what deleted means." Sarcasm bled into Magnus's reply.

It wasn't gone, though. I didn't believe it. "No. Dahlia would save it." She acted like she wanted to forget, but she saved everything. The conversations with Magnus, when Dahlia thought she was gone. The dozens of iterations of this program. Their old apartment preserved perfectly out of time. "Where did she put it?"

Magnus pushed back from her laptop. "I don't know."

"Why not?" I couldn't hide my frustration.

She turned a lethal glare on me. "You're the one fucking her. You're the one she loves. Why don't you know where she put the fucking data?"

I knew fighting with Magnus wasn't the answer, but the urge to take action of any sort was potent.

"This won't get us anywhere." Frey's voice was tight.

"*Holy fuck.*" Magnus's shout echoed in the room. "There aren't always answers. Sometimes life is shitty and then people die, and you let her go. Why did you let her go?"

"We'll find her." We didn't have a choice. *I* didn't have a choice. "She's not dying."

Sinking back in her seat, Magnus clenched her jaw. Unshed tears shone at the edges of her eyes, and she was either going to cry or explode with anger.

I couldn't let her explode. Dahlia would be upset.

"She *can* die. We all can." Magnus's voice was tight. "I've seen it. Even if that wasn't real, it proved death is possible."

This was a waste of time. Dahlia was out there, and we were fighting in here. I didn't want to be reasonable or logical; I wanted to fight. Instead, I crouched in front of Magnus and covered her hand, forcing her gaze to mine.

"You know where she is, because you're her sister," I said. "Yes, I love Dahlia *so much*. But you *know* her. You know how her mind works, in ways I'll never comprehend. You know she's alive now, just like you knew when you were separated from her. If she moved that information, if she tucked answers away anywhere, you know where."

"I don't." The tears in Magnus's eyes were evident in her voice as well.

I would fight anything for Dahlia. *Kill* anything. And I'd beg on her behalf as well. "Please."

Magnus closed her laptop and dropped her head into her hands.

Please don't let her cry. It wouldn't help, and I was so very bad with tears.

The breath Magnus dragged in seemed to temporarily suck all the air from the room. "When we were hunting potentials, we would leave each other messages in books." She opened her laptop again. "Nothing overt. Nothing someone else could look at and figure out. We'd write things on gum wrappers or candy bar wrappers or cookie wrappers..." Her fingers flew over the keyboard.

That sounded so wonderfully Dahlia, but there was a flaw in it all. "You're on the computer, not at the bookshelf," I said.

"The message is almost always a movie reference, and it gets tucked between the pages of a book that has the answer." Magnus didn't seem concerned by my concern.

The two of them spoke to each other in cryptic riddles, and thought it was normal. The gods had influenced them more than they realized.

"We saved copies of all the legit books we found on the dark web." Magnus was almost speaking a foreign language right now. "If she stuck the information in one of those, the file date or the file size or something will have changed, especially if she was in a hurry and wanted an easy way to remember later."

Hurry. I kept the shouted command to myself as Magnus scrolled. And scrolled. And then some more. I balled up my fists and fought the urge to put one or both through the nearest wall.

"It doesn't make sense." Magnus was muttering again. "This is the book that references where the witch took the husband. To the house he lived in before he met the bride. To a life pre-marriage."

If that was about me or Frey, there were more than a dozen of those. A few were no longer standing, but that didn't help. "You said she'd leave a note. What does the note say?"

"*Hunted.* Horrible movie. I have no idea what it means."

I did. "The cabin in Norway. Where I used to hunt."

"Then she would have put *The Hunt.*" Magnus sounded certain.

"No." Realization spread across Frey's face. "Because TOM sent Starkad there, hoping Fen would kill him."

"And then hunted you both." Magnus looked up, eyes wide. "Fuck, that sounds exactly like the kind of place Vidar would wait for her."

Finally. A direction. A way to act. "Let's go."

"We're not walking in there unprepared. We haven't even confirmed that's where she is," Frey said.

"Can you feel the place?" Magnus asked.

Frey closed his eyes and slid into focus, but he wasn't there long. "No. It's a blank spot of nothing."

Magnus wiggled her fingers, showing off the ring Dahlia had made for her. "I can see if she's there. I can't search the whole world quickly, but now that I have a location..." Her pause was barely a heartbeat. Not enough to finish drawing a breath. "She's there. Same world. Different plane."

We agreed there weren't many ways we could prepare for a fight like this, but I gave Magnus a thorough description of the cabin, as well as where the TOM soldiers had waited us out when Starkad and I faced them.

"Even though Dahlia showed up alone, Vidar will know we're coming for her," Magnus said.

I nodded at her ring. "Does he know about that?"

"Hard to say." Magnus stared at her hand and wiggled her fingers. "He may have seen it at Skuld's house. It may be part of a prophecy somewhere."

The odds were against us. I should hate that, but my wolf stalked in my head, ready for whatever came next. "Frey will drop me two kilometers from the house. I'll move in wolf form—small wolf—and meet you at the house five minutes after that."

"If the place is guarded, it won't be heavily." Magnus sounded certain. "There aren't enough TOM soldiers left for Vidar to spread them that thin. Even if he puts all of his people out there, he's got fewer than fifty left."

"If they're all mortal? Not a problem." Possibly too easy given how worked up I was.

"They may have trinkets like this." Magnus displayed the ring again.

Still not worried. I could bite off a finger or a hand without a problem.

"What if Minato is there?" Frey had to go and bring logic into things. "That's who Dahlia went after."

Magnus stood. "Then Minato is focused on keeping Dahlia in the dream."

That was a possibility I didn't want to face.

We phased to the cabin, and my concern cranked higher as I approached and didn't find a single soldier. There was nothing here to fight. Vidar had left the place unguarded.

It took about thirty seconds to clear the property. Frey couldn't feel anyone. I couldn't smell them.

Except Dahlia and Minato. They were here.

I followed the scents to find Minato sleeping in one room, the bracer from the siren on her wrist.

And Dahlia lay in the next room. She was Snow White. Still. Lifeless but breathing, with pale skin and dark hair. Except a kiss wouldn't pull her from this slumber.

"Yank her out," Magnus said. "Get her out of there and we can kill Minato, just like in the story."

Frey reached for Dahlia, and I grabbed his wrist. The look he gave me spoke to every conflicted thought in my head. If he didn't try we could lose her. If he did try, I could lose him.

"I have to do something," Frey said. "Keep me grounded."

I had no idea how to do that, but I was going to anyway. "All right."

Frey knelt next to Dahlia and took her hand.

Magnus guarded the door, and I kept one eye on the same entrance, and the rest of my attention on Frey. If he showed signs of slipping, I was prepared to yank him out and fuck him against the wall to make him whole again.

This was different than in the past, because Dahlia lay still, rather than trying to attack. That would make things easier.

Wouldn't it?

Seconds ticked away. Dahlia muttered in her sleep and kicked one foot, but didn't otherwise stir.

"Come on, damn you." Frey's voice was low and his tone desperate.

A chill passed over me, and then another, and I shivered. The temperature had dropped rapidly in here, and the cold radiated from Frey and Dahlia.

"This isn't good." Magnus glanced at them, before giving her full attention to the entrance again.

Frey murmured strings of unintelligible phrases. I caught the occasional word in our original tongue, but not enough to catch the meaning.

The frustration in his voice, though. The slide toward anger and then something darker, was obvious. When he roared, "*Wake up, damn you,*" in our native language, Dahlia didn't move.

I yanked Frey back, breaking the contact between him and Dahlia.

"I wasn't done." Darkness dripped from his words. "I *will* save her."

"No." I crushed my mouth to his, capturing him and pouring all my love for him into the kiss.

Frey went slack against my touch. When he shoved me back, I was startled. "Yes." His growl matched anything I could summon. "She's part of us and we're not losing her to this."

I swore I felt the darkness and fury rolling from him. My wolf wanted to play, because that kind of rage meant battle.

This wasn't the time. "If you sacrifice yourself, it won't matter if you save her. You're both idiots," I said.

"Make a decision," Magnus barked. "Or watch the door so I can."

"There's no other choice." Frey turned to Dahlia again.

But there was. We'd spent so much time finding a way to fight this creature, and we were using none of it. "There's another way." I stalked into the room next door, to Minato's sleeping form, and tore her hand off, separating the bracer from her.

Her scream was the stuff of nightmares.

Good.

"Kill her. Smart." Magnus stepped in, sword drawn.

I angled my body between her and Minato, and cursed myself for having to protect the Baku. "We can't until we know for certain it won't trap Dahlia in the dream. Besides," I held up Minato's severed hand. "Now we have this, and I'm going to wear it. I don't care how much it hurts."

I grasped the bracer tightly, and a pain like I'd never known seared through my hand and then my body. I clenched my jaw and yanked, despite the red licking the edge of my vision.

The pain stopped abruptly.

What the...?

The bracer lay on the floor at my feet, and my fingers were gone. They grew back quickly, but it hurt almost as badly as picking up the bracer. I reached for it again and Frey stopped me.

"If you can't hold it, trying over and over will only weaken you." He sounded as enraged, as pained, as I felt.

I wanted to argue, but he had a point.

So what were we supposed to do?

CHAPTER 27
DAHLIA

If I ever made it out of here, I was never going to hear the end of it from Magnus, Frey, and Fen.

Not that I knew where *here* was. I got the ping. I hid the information so they couldn't come after me and get killed, and I moved to the location.

Or that was what I meant to do.

But then I was in a dream. One of these fucking hyper real iterations from Minato where time was irrelevant and everything was like 8K television, with the sharpness turned up too high.

"There are days I wonder if you're actually mine." Vidar's condescension hit my back and clawed its way over me.

I spun to find we were in his office on campus. Or a dream recreation of it. He stood near the bookshelves, and I was abruptly seated in a chair. One of the high-backed wooden ones that was grossly uncomfortable, and I suspected intentionally so. "Is that something gods do? Fake paternity? Do you actually care who else Skuld fucked?"

"No." Vidar strolled toward me. While he was moving at a normal speed, the walk seemed to take forever.

Fucking dreams.

He finally stopped in front of me, pressed his hands into mine on the arms of the chair and leaned in, putting him distinctly in my personal space.

I tried to wriggle free, but my limbs didn't move. I wouldn't let my fear show. I wouldn't. I wouldn't.

"You're not going to ask what this is all about?" His sneer was too close. Too real.

I made my shrug look as casual as possible. "Don't care."

"Perfect." He straightened up again. "Because I want to tell you, and you're going to sit there and listen, not because I need you to know, but to irritate the fuck out of you. Think of it as repaying the favor."

Invisible bonds strapped me into the seat, and suddenly I was trapped in A Clockwork Orange. "At least you know your talking is torture." I forced my tone to sound light. "Quite self-aware of you for a god."

He made a *tsk* sound and moved to the window. When he opened the blinds, NEON sat on the other side. Not a NEON I'd ever seen though. This was broken. Dust-covered. Light spilled in through cracks in the roof. The stage had gaping dips in it.

I swallowed a whimper.

"You could have come to me, when you realized you were Skuld's replacement," he said. "I would have built you up. Made you into a ruler."

What? "And you could've told me at any time during school *Hey, I'm your baby-daddy. I know this whole forced assassination thing sucks, but you could be working for me instead.* There was a point in my life where I was young and impressionable, and would have bowed to anyone who was nice to me."

Thank fuck I'd learned better.

"No." Was that amusement in Vidar's voice? "I've already told you, you were the runt of the litter. The disappointment. You didn't deserve this position. But I can't fucking kill you myself. I don't know why not, but I have tried. You think I just let you be, and haven't been acting this entire time?"

"So instead you're torturing me?" Huh. I could see it. Fuckwit.

He shrugged. "Pushing you until you fuck up. But you are so fucking stubborn and hard to break. I cannot figure out where you got it from."

Why did the gods always have the most convoluted plans? "I certainly didn't learn it from watching you."

"I doubt you've learned anything from me.

Perhaps I should have appealed to your softer side. Approached you in a tone you would better understand?" Snideness dripped from his words.

Like that, we were on the Death Star instead of in his office. The widow behind The Emperor's throne still looked out over NEON though. Vidar wore a long black cloak with a hood, and was Palpatine pre-Mace Windu fight. "Everything that has transpired has done so according to my design. Your friends are walking into a trap, and I'm quite safe from them. When they arrive, they'll be unable to wake you, and will join you in eternal slumber."

Ugh. He couldn't even write his own lines, he had to go and quote Star Wars. Gross.

"So one," I cut him off. "That dude was a dick, and never once made a convincing argument. Luke was a whiny idiot, and how dare you compare me to him? And also, if you're going to play on my daddy issues, you need to be Darth Vader. Come on, you're practically named after him."

Like that, Vidar was himself again, and the setting was a void, aside from the large picture window looking out over a rapidly deteriorating NEON. And then the windows expanded to fill every available wall. I was trapped in a dome of destroyed NEON.

"Fine. We'll do this the way you want," Vidar said. "I can't kill you, but a Baku can trap a dragon in a dream for a long time. Loki didn't give you the real knife. No one but you can wear the bracer. Urd or Artura I suppose, but they've written you off. Your friends will never pull you out of this dream."

That was a bullshit taunt if I'd ever heard one.

He turned his back to me, and paused. "By the way, you're the reason I could get Minato into NEON. It doesn't matter if you deny the shared bloodline, you're still attached to me. I always know where you are. I'm always capable of getting to you. It's just more fun to let you think you have a chance."

I lunged with a roar, but he was already gone.

There was nothing again. Nothing but the thought *this was my fault.* NEON was gone because of me. Frey was breaking because of me. Because I saved the evil dream cunt queen, then couldn't fight her off myself. So I made Frey take me in. Made Fen protect me.

Magnus was hurt because even as a dragon, I couldn't stop our enemies.

And now all three of them were going to come after me, because I thought I could save them, and all I'd done was fucked things up worse.

I was at the edge of a room. Magnus's room, next door to Frey and Fen's apartment. She sat on her bed, back to the wall and knees pulled to her chest. The way she stared into nothingness, she hadn't noticed me.

Tears rolled silently down her face. She didn't

move, not even a shake or a shudder, but her whimper tore at my heart.

I tried to walk toward her. To pull her into my arms and comfort her. To cry with her.

But I couldn't move, because this wasn't a dream, this was a memory. From barely a week ago when I'd found her like this.

I said her name, again and again, until it synced up with the memory.

She looked up at the sound of my voice. "I can't right now," Magnus said.

"You don't have to do anything." I'd wanted to reassure her then and I still wanted that now.

Magnus shifted her head to stare at the wall again. "You do. I need you to go."

And I did. I should've stayed. The voice in my head insisted she needed me there. Why hadn't I stayed?

Because she didn't want me there, and it was my fault she was going through this.

That's not your voice, it's Vidar's. Hel's.

Another memory, fainter though it was more recent, murmured in my mind. I was in the hallway at NEON, a few feet from Frey's office. He had to know I was out here, because he knew everything about this place, but neither he nor Fen had paused in their conversation.

I should have announced my presence, but when I approached and heard them arguing, I froze. Minato's name was in there. Mine. It was a list of everything that had gone wrong recently.

The memory was recent too. Neither of them blamed me, but they didn't need to. This was all my fault.

The memories cascaded, one on top of another, all of them falling in the last twelve or so months. It was all terrible. It's as all because I couldn't—

What was this? The scene had changed again, but this wasn't a memory. It was a dream overlapped with a dragon vision. I recognized both sensations.

I also recognized the dead figures on the floor in front of me—Frey, Fen, and an empty spot that was probably Magnus. They lay in the middle of a cabin that looked familiar. Why?

And why was I sleeping on the bed next to them?

CHAPTER 28
FREYR

There was no other option to save Dahlia. Given the damage Fen did to Minato, once Dahlia was conscious we could destroy the Baku. "I'll try again. I will pull her out."

"No." Fen's voice was hard. "I won't lose one of you to save the other. Period."

Then I'd find a way to recover. "What other options do we have?"

"Something. Not this," Fen said.

"Uh... guys?" The sharp injection of worry into Magnus's voice drew my attention, and I followed her gaze to Minato.

Who was staring at us—through us—with glassy eyes. Though her lids were open, I wasn't sure she was awake. The more concerning thing was that her hand had grown back.

Magnus snapped in front of Minato's face, and

the Baku didn't move. Not even to blink or follow the movement.

"Fuck this." Magnus reached for the bracer.

I grabbed for her wrist to stop her, but she'd already grabbed the leather and was fitting it on. Pain was etched across her face, but she still held the bracer.

The cabin vanished, and I was back in NEON. It was as if I'd phased there, all three of us, because Fen and Magnus were here too. However, this wasn't NEON from now. This was NEON nearly a year ago, because Minato was dancing on stage, and Dahlia had joined her.

I knew this night. It was when Dahlia had come to us asking for refuge. Fen should be watching her from the doorway, but he was next to me.

"Are you both real?" Magnus poked Fen in the arm.

He grunted and brushed her finger away. "Would you believe me if I said *yes*? Are you real?"

Was this my dream? Dahlia's? I didn't feel any sort of fear or anything else for Magnus to feed from. At least, no more than my existing worry for Dahlia.

The dance ended, and the women exited the stage. I knew what happened next, and I needed to see if things would play out the same way here. I headed to the back of the stage. No one in the room took notice of me. Of us. Every patron was focused on their own lives.

I found Dahlia behind the curtain, wearing mostly nothing, and talking to me. It was strange to see this from a third person perspective, but it was playing out exactly the way I remembered.

"Why were you up there?" Other-me demanded of Dahlia.

No. This wasn't right. We'd flirted. The conversation had been seductive.

"Minato asked for a favor. I was..." Dahlia trailed off with a frown. "What?"

Other-me grabbed her arm, jostling her entire frame when he shoved her against the wall. "Answer my question, or pay the price." He pressed in closely to her.

Fear curdled in my gut. This was like with the siren. *He* was. But the scene was wrong. Did she remember things this way? Was this Minato's manipulation?

"I was helping. It's never been an issue before." Dahlia sounded terrified.

Other me gripped her arm harder, and she yelped in pain. This Dahlia had still been mortal. "Stop. You're going to break her arm." I was talking to a dream, and I didn't care. I refused to watch this.

Except that Dahlia looked directly at me, fear and confusion splashed on her face.

Other-me jerked her harder. "Look at me. We're not done." His voice was harsh.

Was this my nightmare?

"Imposter." Fen lunged at other me, and sailed right through him.

Magnus grunted, stalked forward with a wicked looking blade appearing in her hand, and sliced at other me.

I should be worried, but I was relieved. That visage of me should not exist.

Magnus's attack was as ineffective as Fen's.

None of this made sense. Was it a dream? A twisted memory? Were all of us here? Were some of us just someone's imagination? I reached for Dahlia when other me did, and she jerked from both of us.

"That's not how it happened," I said. "That's not me."

Are you certain?

Was that Minato's voice?

"It doesn't matter." Dahlia was talking to herself, not us. "That night was a mistake. I made so many mistakes. I should've... Why am I such an idiot?"

"You're not," I said at the same time that other me said, "That's a good question."

Magnus grabbed my arm, and I jumped at the contact. She was holding onto Fen as well. "This isn't real. We are." Her tone was firm and certain. The bracer was still on her wrist, though it seemed to flicker and fade into and out of view. "*She* is. I can feel it."

"Great. What do we do about it?" Fen asked.

Magnus shrugged. "In the fairy tale, the bride

convinces the groom it's all fake, and pulls him out of the dream, right? If you both believe me, we just have to convince her."

"This never happened to me." Dahlia was watching us. "I don't understand."

The scenery changed again, and we were in a place I didn't recognize. An apartment I'd never seen before. The decor was basic, but the random splashes of color were distinctly Dahlia and Magnus.

Both women whimpered. "*No*," Magnus muttered. "Not this one, please."

Dahlia had moved with us, but there was another Magnus here as well. Both of them wore jeans and white T-shirts. What Dahlia referred to as TOM standard apparel.

"I don't understand how you could do this." Dream-Magnus managed both taunting and distraught in the same statement. "This is our family. They're a just couple of fuck-boys."

Real-Magnus coughed, as if clearing her throat, and blushed bright red. "I mean, not *just*." She glanced at Fen and me.

"They're safe. They don't lie to us. Vidar fucking lies to us. Bragi. We promised each other." Dahlia's scowl was etched deeply across her face.

Dream-Magnus stalked closer. "That was with Hel. This is different. *This* is home."

"I'm sorry," Real-Magnus whispered. "I was so wrong." She seemed to be talking to herself.

"This is fucked up." Fen's words mimicked mine. Was this some twisted version of the past, modified to feed their trauma? Or was this how it had happened?

Who needed to create nightmares when the reality had already been enough to scar Dahlia and Magnus?

Dahlia sank to the floor. "At least we would've been safe if we'd stayed."

"No." I stalked toward her, Fen at my side, and pulled her to her feet. "You would have been dead."

She looked through me, but then focused on me. "But you wouldn't have been. NEON would still be standing."

Did she know we were really here? Did she think she was talking to a dream? I wasn't sure if asking her would make things better or worse.

"You can't say how things would have played out if you stayed here," Fen said. "But you don't know that it would have been better, and I wouldn't give up any of our time together."

She gave a bitter laugh. "I've tried to kill you. I almost did." She looked around. "This didn't happen. You're making shitty dreams if you think this is going to make me change how I think," Dahlia shouted at the air.

"We're not dreams." I wasn't, anyway. And I had to believe Magnus that all three of us were real, or I'd slowly lose my sanity. "We're actually here."

"Uh-huh." The way Dahlia huffed carried hints of surrender. "That sounds like something a dream would say."

"That also sounds like something a real person would say." Fen pointed out.

Real-Magnus huffed and stalked forward, walking right through herself. "I wasn't right then," she crouched and put herself at eye level with Dahlia. "I may not be right now. I don't fucking know, but don't do this. Don't be me."

What?

The way Dahlia frowned, not with confusion but with concern, made me think she understood Magnus's reference. "But what about—?"

"Nothing." Magnus said. "What about nothing. Do *not* sit here and give up because we have some bad memories. You're smarter than that. And I'm not talking about *you're such a smart girl, why don't you do better?* Fuck that noise. Stop being a self-centered brat, and snap out of it."

Fen growled and I placed myself between him and Magnus. "I don't think this is—"

"Self-centered?" Dahlia talked over me. She was on her feet now. "I'm here for you. To keep you all safe."

Dream-Magnus was still holding half of a different conversation, but real-Magnus stood toe-to-toe with Dahlia. "You're here so you don't have to watch us suffer."

"Exactly," Dahlia said. "To save you."

"To punish yourself," Magnus countered. "Because that's what I would've done if I'd had a chance.

Dahlia poked her. "You sound like Magnus. Then again, so does she." Dahlia looked around the room again. "This is getting stupid. Pick an angle and stick to it at least through a single torture scene," she shouted into the air.

"*Hey*." Magnus returned the poke, jabbing Dahlia in the chest with a long, clawed ring. "Don't give that cunt credit for my anger. Fuck her."

The way Dahlia's expression shifted, from frustration to disbelief to an almost-smile, was disconcerting. She grabbed Magnus's wrist and examined the ring. "She's not wearing the one from Vidar."

"Of course I'm not. Fuck that guy," Real-Magnus said.

But Dahlia was looking past her, to Dream-Magnus who continued to hold up half a conversation, despite there being no response. "I hated that day, because you were wearing that fucking ring. Because part of me wanted to believe Vidar bought you with that thing, and the rest of me hated myself for even having the thought."

"He didn't. I would've stayed regardless, and I would've been wrong regardless. Just like you are now." Magnus wasn't pulling any punches.

Dahlia continued to examine Magnus's ring.

"Every single detail is right," Dahlia sounded amazed.

"Because it's the real thing. Just like this." Magnus held up the arm with the bracer. "Which, by the way, this thing is killing me. Are you ready to leave with us?"

So many people put their focus solely on romance and sex when it came to love, but watching Dahlia and Magnus together, it was clear their bond was different, though just as potent, as any two people who were madly in love with each other.

I couldn't imagine one of them existing without the other any more than I wanted to be without Fen. Or Dahlia.

And I *did* love Dahlia. I needed her out of this place—us out of this place—so I could tell her. She needed to be a part of our lives. Forever.

"Let's go kill a bitch." Magnus grabbed my hand and Fen's, and Dahlia was already holding onto her arm.

Magnus vanished, and so did the apartment scene.

"What just happened?" I asked.

Dahlia gave a brief shake of her head. "I think she left without us." A pained look crossed her face, and a scream tore from her throat that would likely haunt me for decades. She vanished in a blink and Magnus was back. But the bracer was gone.

Before I could ask what happened, our environment changed again. Flame licked at the walls, and in the background screams bounced in the air. There was no distinct shape to anything, unlike in Dahlia's dreams.

"Get down." Fen was already bounding toward me, shifting to a wolf as he moved, and leaping over my head at something behind me.

Chaos erupted around us. Creatures I hadn't seen in centuries, or had only heard stories about, swarmed in and attacked us. It was instinct for me to throw up a wall to keep them out, but some of them broke through without pause. The instant I closed one fracture in the shield, another appeared.

Fen and Magnus were in full-fight mode, with him as a wolf and her in her Valkyrie form. They slashed and bit and tore at everything that flew at us, and each time, they took out the threat milliseconds before one of us was hit.

"What's going on?" I asked.

Neither of them answered, both being too involved in the battle.

"Oh, no." Dahlia's voice came from beside me, startling me.

She was back, and this time she wore the bracer. "We need to leave." She grabbed my hand.

No need to tell me twice. "Fen. Magnus. To us."

Neither of them

Dahlia and I reached for them, but with each grasp, they were just out of range.

"*Fen.*" I made his name rattle in the room.

He didn't so much as flinch or glance in my direction.

"*Magnus.*" Dahlia didn't have any more luck. She took my hand again. "We'll come back for them. I promise."

I had no doubt.

She and I appeared in the cabin again, next to where she'd been sleeping. Magnus was on the bed now, instead. "This is how I found her," Dahlia said. "You and Fen were in the other room, with Minato. I think Magnus put the bracer on me, and..." She gestured vaguely. "What now?"

Now we needed to do the same thing as when we'd arrived—make sure everyone was conscious, then kill Minato. "I pull them out."

"No."

I was getting a little tired of hearing that. "Is there another way?"

Dahlia scowled. "There has to be."

"There's not, and we're out of time." My trick hadn't worked with Dahlia, but after seeing her dreams I suspected I knew why. She was drowning in guilt, but I didn't know that she'd let her passions consume her. With Fen, with Magnus, it looked like that was exactly what was keeping them trapped. His love of the fight and her hatred for... So much.

I found Fen in the other room, as Dahlia said, and carried him in to lay him on the floor next to the bed Magnus was in. Keeping them apart, in case one of them thrashed or became otherwise animated in their sleep, seemed wise.

"Please don't," Dahlia said.

There was no other choice. I placed my hands on Fen's face, and did the one thing I never wanted—the only thing worse than this would be seeing him die—I grasped the threads of passion that bound us, and I muted them.

I smothered the love that tied us together, and choked out that connection of passion that drove me when it came to Fen.

This wasn't right. It wasn't fair. I shouldn't have to do this. Rage crept in, white-hot and vivid.

I couldn't keep going without Fen. Without Dahlia. But was it worth it to be here, if I couldn't love them anymore. I didn't lov—

No. I'd burn the world to the ground if I had to give up what I felt for them. I was doing that now—surrendering. Suffocating the love Fen felt for me.

What was I supposed to do? If I didn't pull him out, he was lost forever. If I did, he was lost to me forever. Which price was I willing to pay? Keep his love or keep his life?

I'd destroy everything if I lost either one

CHAPTER 29

DAHLIA

Save us, please. Magnus's voice echoed in my head as Frey turned an angry roar on me, fury etched across his features.

I had learned to do so much. Despite what Vidar or Artura or anyone thought, I was powerful. The ability to piss off and sometimes even destroy mystical beings spilled inside me.

But I couldn't do this. Not alone. Not life. Not this fight. Not saving my best friend and the men I loved. I needed them in order to save them. Despite everything they tried to drill into us at TOM, over and over, I was pretty sure needing them wasn't a bad thing.

How was I supposed to help Frey in return though? With rage contorting his face and licking from him like flames, I swore I felt his despair. It was cloying.

I didn't want to lose him to this. Not when we were just starting to admit we loved each other. When we were barely at the point of figuring things out. I'd only had Magnus back for a few weeks. I'd only been able to love Fen for a few months.

Fuck this. Vidar wasn't taking this from him. I refused to let him or Minato or anyone remove the things I loved from the world.

I wouldn't die fighting them. Instead, I would show them I knew how to live, in spite of them.

"Frey." Fear quaked inside me, but I wouldn't let it—wouldn't let them—win. Besides, I didn't need to be afraid of Frey, only what would happen if we lost him.

The look he gave me was skinned and scraped and tortured fury. "Don't."

But I would. I pressed my back to Frey's chest and pulled his arms tight around me. Even when I was terrified or feeling lost, I always felt safe here.

"I love you too." Though I'd said that to Fen hundreds of times, it hit me differently when I directed it at Frey. It was a new lift in my heart.

While he'd never said it directly, the siren did, and he'd confirmed. He tightened his grip around me.

I should keep talking. Keep feeling. I didn't want this to be about sex, but I wasn't going to tuck away everything that made my pulse race and my heart happy and my world brighter. "I love other things too. Not that it's the same kind of love. But the fact that we have breakfast on a different balcony every morning, and that you have a bartender who instinctively knows what each person wants to drink, and sunrises, and stupid superhero movies that have no idea what real gods are like, and my Docs, and Lady Gaga."

I couldn't stop. The list reeled through my brain. Everything that made me happy. Everything that gave me a reason to look forward to the next minutes in life. As I ticked off items, I felt a tug inside. A cord behind my heart that tightened with each new item. That made me feel closer to Frey and almost wrapped around both of us.

We were standing in the middle of a remote cabin, with the people I loved sleeping next to us, impossible to wake up, and a creature in the other room that I would incinerate in a heartbeat if I could, and I was listing the things that made me feel like a Disney Princess.

"And Fen," I said. "I love Fen. And Magnus." The pain was still there from thinking I'd lost her. That urge to burn to the world in her name. That drive to make everyone suffer who had wronged her. I'd still do that. I'd find Vidar. Bragi. Nico, if he didn't pull his head out of his ass and remember her.

"And you." Apparently I was still going. "I love you for teaching me not all gods are assholes. For your patience, and your skill, and for saving Fen, and—"

"Stop." Frey pressed his lips into the top of my head, and I felt the word whisper through my hair. "I know. You love a lot of things."

Was he mad? Was I ruining the moment? He didn't sound mad.

"It's one of the things that makes you so addictive," he said softly. "The gods themselves tried to beat you down, and you still find something to like —something to be passionate about—in so much of your world. If I could harness that, maybe I could save them."

"I'm always happy to share." Did I just say that? I was such a fucking dork. But could I? Was it really that dumb? "We work together so well when we stop fighting ourselves. Against the siren. When we dance. When we fuck."

Frey's chuckle rolled through me. "I have no idea how you do that."

"Because I'm a magical fucking dragon."

He spun me to face him, and grasped my hands. "Yeah, you are. Everything that TOM tried to beat out of you, that Artura scolded you for... You never lost who you are. Do you know how rare that is? To appreciate life so much—to be so passionate about the world—that you always know who you are?"

I didn't know how to respond to that, so I shrugged shyly.

He kissed me on the forehead. "Do me a favor and keep thinking about the things that make you happy."

"Ooh, like Peter Pan." Yup, I was a total dork.

He shook his head. "I was thinking more like Julie Andrews, but whatever works for you. Especially if it's something you'd fight for. Something that consumes your heart when you think about it. And don't stop me unless I slip again."

I could do that. I actually didn't know if I could do anything else, because now that I'd started down this path, so many images flooded in. Running through the forest with Fen chasing me. Sniping digital baddies with Magnus in our favorite game. Every time Frey and I got to choreograph a new dance.

He didn't let go of my hand when he took Fen's again.

I felt despair lick the edges of my soul. If they were all gone, like now, what was the point?

But I wouldn't let that happen. The world would not take this from me. I clung to every single good memory, and even some of the bad ones, especially if they ended with sex or ice cream.

Fen's eyelids fluttered, and he grunted. His eyes flew open, and he sat straight up.

Was he trapped in a dream, like the patrons in NEON had been? Would we have to fight him?

I couldn't fight Fen. Wouldn't fight Fen.

"Am I awake?" he asked.

Frey pulled him further upright. "I don't know how to answer that. Take Dahlia's hand."

Fen frowned, but did what Frey said.

So far so good. I mean, I felt a little ridiculous, everyone holding hands like in a cheesy movie, where thinking positive saves the day. All I had to do was think positive things, instead of fighting, and we'd be all right.

I didn't care how ludicrous it was, because Fen was back, and soon Magnus would be too.

Frey grasped Magnus's hand and an eerie hush settled into the room.

Any minute now, the same thing would happen to her that happened to Fen. She'd stir. She'd growl. She'd be awake.

Despair licked the edges of my mind, and my enthusiasm ebbed.

I pushed back, and turned my focus to Frey. He needed me to be... me? What did that even mean? I tried to grasp the thoughts I'd had before. About everything I loved.

Seconds ticked away, and time slowed to a crawl. Nothing was happening. Magnus wasn't moving beyond the slow, steady rise and fall of her chest with each breath.

Frey's expression was twisting toward anger again, and I pushed past my own frustration.

Fen didn't look happy either. His growl was terrifying, and his grip tightened on my hand.

It wasn't working.

"You need to stop," Fen warned.

Frey shook his head. "No." The word landed hard. Angry. "I have to do this."

No. This wasn't right. Why wasn't she waking up? Why wouldn't she leave the dream with us before? Why wasn't she coming back to me?

What was I going to do in a world without my sister?

I tore my hands free from Frey and Fen, pushed Frey back, and knelt next to Magus. I didn't want to give into this feeling, but it was so familiar and fresh. This was a month ago all over again, when I thought Magnus was dead. When I hurt so very much.

I didn't realize I was crying until a tear landed on my hand. And then another. I pressed my forehead to Magnus's, and let the tears fall. "You can't leave me. Not again. I don't want my world to not have you in it, and I swear if you leave me alone, bitch, I will haunt your ghosts until the end of the earth."

Who gave a fuck if that didn't make sense? None of this was right anyway, and Magnus was still asleep.

She muttered and her head rolled. "Ugh. Why is my face all wet?" Her voice was tight and weak.

And it was the most glorious sound ever. I pulled

back enough to see her opening her eyes. As she tried to sit up, I hugged her tightly and pulled her upright.

"You came back to me." I was insane and laughing through my tears.

"I almost didn't," Magnus said. "I was…" She shook her head. "We have a Baku to kill."

Right. Happy reunions later. I hopped to my feet and tugged her up too.

"You're an idiot, by the way." Magnus rolled her neck and stretched. "If I'm the dead one, how are *you* going to haunt *me*?"

I stuck my tongue out at her.

"*Ladies, are we killing something?*" Fen's voice was in my head, because he was already in wolf form.

Damn straight we were.

I wanted some kick ass background music to play, ala The Final Battle, as we reached for the door.

Instead, as we stepped into the hallway we were swarmed by hundreds of tiny creatures that looked like Tinker Bell. With teeth as big as their head. One bit me, and then another, and then a dozen more.

"Ow. *Fuck.*" I tried to swat them away. Everyone else was dealing with the same. The bites healed instantly but the swarm was so dense, we couldn't move, and one bite after another wore on us quickly.

Fen lunged and caught several in his mouth, returning the favor of biting. Magnus had a flaming sword in her hand, and she swiped through several others. They singed away and floated to the ground like ash, but there seemed to be no end to the onslaught.

"*Go. Take care of Minato.*" Fen attacked another group of winged-teeth.

I wanted to move, but my feet were frozen to the ground. The scene I was witnessing was like in the shared dream, but this time I could see what Fen and Magnus were fighting.

"Dahlia." Frey grabbed my arm.

Right. Everyone did their job in a fight like this, and those two could handle themselves. If wolves could actually smile, I was pretty sure Fen was grinning ear to ear right now.

I cast a wall of flame in front of myself, and Frey and I walked the short distance to the room where Minato lay.

Fen and Magnus rushed into the room a moment after we did, and closed the door. Frey snapped, putting a shield up between us and the other side, and the sound of thousands of gnashing teeth echoed through the door.

Minato lay on the bed, still sleeping, looking as peaceful and innocent as the day I first met her.

Such bullshit.

I had no idea which weapon would kill her, but I had the letter opener from Skuld's house and the blade from Loki. *Please let it be one of these.* Both were imbued with dragon energy—I could *feel* it—and the letter opener was far more powerful than its appearance implied.

I sliced both across her neck, to take her head off. Or as near to it as possible.

Minato's eyes flew open as the wounds healed instantly, and she lunged at me with a hiss.

Fuck. I leaped back as much out of instinct as anything.

"Don't touch her." With a wave of Frey's hand, Minato stalled, bound by invisible restraints.

She broke free in a blink, but Magnus had already summoned a spear and stabbed her through the foot, pinning her to the ground.

Fen leaped past Magnus, knocked Minato back, and pinned her to the ground.

And I was sitting on my ass doing nothing. *Get up, me. Get up and fight.*

"Move," Frey ordered.

Fen bounded aside, and when Minato chased, she slammed into an invisible wall. She was trapped in a box, similar to what Frey had used on the siren.

"It's already cracking." Warning bled from Frey's words.

I knew what to do. I stalked toward the invisible box, just recognizing the waver of its outline, like heat off the asphalt, and walked through the side Minato was trying to break.

She stared at me in disbelief.

"Do you think if I finally finish. my contract and

kill you, that Vidar will finally love me?" I didn't know why I asked the question, but it felt like so much had led up to it.

Minato scoffed. "What? You delusional—"

The box filled with flame, consuming both of us. This was the hottest I could make it, and it consumed her in a blink, turning her to ash.

As the walls of Frey's box fell away, the flame evaporated.

"We're coming for you next, Daddy." I screamed into the air.

Magnus smacked me in the arm. "You're such a fucking dork."

I was. Proudly and unapologetically. "Takes one to know one."

Was it really over? I'd felt Minato die. I'd extinguished that life. She was gone.

I was barely aware of Frey and Fen taking my hand and Magnus's, until the room vanished and we appeared in the apartment.

"If you *ever* do something like that again..." Frey whirled on me.

I scrunched up my nose. The stress and adrenaline were sinking too fast for me to be serious. "You'll spank me?" A huge weight had been lifted. This felt good.

"*Ugh*. At least wait until I'm out of the room?" Magnus's disgust was exaggerated.

My laugh slipped out, and once I started I

couldn't stop. This wasn't funny, but I was so relieved.

The laughter died quickly, and we all seemed to collapse into each other. The war wasn't over, but this battle finally was. And I'd gotten lucky. Luckier than anyone else ever. Because I'd come out of it with the people who mattered.

I wouldn't change any of this for the world. Being snuggled between Frey and Fen. Having Magnus laying across my legs. I adored all of this so much. As long as I had them, my sister and the men I loved, I could take on the entire world.

CHAPTER 30
FREYR

As the high of victory became muted, a somber mood settled into the room. Not in a bad way. More in a *we can finally rest now* way.

There were still things lost, but what we had, what I had, was incredible.

"I should go." Magnus stood. "I need to talk to Nico again. To try again."

Dahlia scrambled to her feet. "I'll—"

"Stay here." Magnus squeezed her hand. "I'll be back, I promise."

"You'd better be." Dahlia gave her a long hug, then let go so Magnus could walk out the front door.

Looking down at herself, Dahlia tugged on the hem of her shirt with pout. "And this was one of my favorites."

Was she really trying to elicit sympathy for that?

"What?" Dahlia met my gaze.

I must have let my disbelief show.

"Then maybe next time don't run off alone to fight the bad guys," Fen said.

Her lower lip jutted out further. "The shirt would've gotten torn regardless."

This was cute. Playful. Fun. "One of us might have reminded you not to wear it." Though unlikely it would've been Fen. Or me. "Magnus, for instance."

"I did it to save all of you." Actual sheepish apology trickled into Dahlia's reply.

I gripped the back of her neck, reveling in the electricity that sped between us, and crushed my mouth to hers. If I could do that again and again, with her, with Fen, it wouldn't be enough. That wouldn't stop me from trying, though. Fen was my heart, but Dahlia was tied to both of our souls. "We couldn't have beaten Minato unless we were all there. Do you know that now?"

She nodded, and her pout vanished.

"I'm sorry about the shirt. I can send it to The Tailor, if you'd like," I offered. "But for tonight, I think we need to clean off from the fight."

I blinked us into the bathroom with the comment. Usually we walked from place to place in our own home, but there was an urgency I couldn't ignore. I planted us next to the giant, jetted bathtub and turned to Dahlia.

Her clothing was tattered and her hair was

mussed, hanging wildly around her dirt-smeared face.

She was stunning.

I removed her clothing slowly, laying kisses along each new piece of exposed skin. Her shoulders. Her chest. Her breasts, and then her thighs.

Somehow—years of practice presumably—Fen managed to remove my clothes at the same time.

"I want to take someone's clothes off," Dahlia said playfully, between gasps and moans induced by my kisses.

"You didn't need me for your big bad fight," Fen teased. "Now that you want a second big naked man, I'm important again?"

Dahlia moved closer to my mouth with each kiss. "Duh."

They fed off each other so well. Their humor. Their ease together. I loved every bit of it.

"Maybe I'll make you keep your hands off me." If Fen thought his threat was effective, I suspected Dahlia was about to prove him wrong.

No one made her do anything she didn't want to.

"I can do a lot without touching you," she countered.

His snort of disbelief turned to a yelp, and I glanced over my shoulder to see he was naked now.

Dahlia must have done that magically. She'd come so far from those early days when she'd discovered she was a dragon. It was incredible to see.

Fen fisted his cock. "Are you going to suck this without touching it, too?"

A glance at Dahlia and her thoughtful expression said she was considering it. "I could, but no one would enjoy that very much."

She made a good point.

"In the tub, both of you." I urged them toward the water.

I tried to keep them focused on cleaning each other. Soap and water and ebbing adrenaline made for a lot of silly seduction, and I was here for it. But I also took a few cautious moments to check both of my loves and make sure they were intact. I no longer trusted our invulnerabilities to be reliable.

Each time Fen or I brushed a touch over Dahlia, especially a sensitive spot, she made the softest, sweetest sounds.

The longer we cleaned, the rougher Fen's touches became. He was restraining himself and tired of it. I didn't blame him—with everything we'd been through, he was looking for a physical outlet.

So was I.

And this was why I needed both him and Dahlia —their different passions. It was also why Dahlia was able to help me wake up Fen. Her passion was so pure and genuine that when she loved something— someone—there were no apologies. She just *loved*.

She added a layer to our life that made us better and stronger.

I pulled her into my lap, but didn't penetrate her yet. I wanted to hold her next to me. To tease her and have her as close as possible.

Dahlia giggled and squirmed, pressing more of her weight into me. "But Mr. Freyr, I Just got all clean and now you're getting dirty."

Fen knelt in front of her and gripped her chin to look her in the eye. His growl was low and delicious. "Duckie-dragon, you have no idea what dirty is."

"I have a little bit of an idea."

Fen stood, and water slid off him, leaving his handsome, built frame glistening in the lights. *Creation,* he was sexy. He was also rock hard, his erection standing as straight as he was. He glided his hand to the back of her head, and pulled her into him as he thrust his hips toward her.

She wrapped her lips around his cock without protest, gasps of pleasure drifting from both of them.

When they were like this, I could feed off them for hours.

Doing so would make me stronger, but it wouldn't get me off. With Fen fucking Dahlia's face, I slipped my fingers between her legs.

She gasped and her body jerked when I brushed her clit, but she resumed her sucking with consistent enthusiasm.

I stroked her while she did the same for Fen, and let their desires roll over and through me. The love in this room was so intense, it was like a fine wine. They were both close to orgasm, and Fen was holding back. I hit the right spot with Dahlia, based on her gasp and pause, and I homed in on repeating the motion, the pressure.

I circled her clit until she was gasping around Fen's shaft, and grinding in my lap. With a little more attention, she fell into climax. Each spasm of her body was delicious. Each grunt of pleasure was another word of worship.

She was so slick, it was easy to slide inside her, even in the water. With my cock buried inside her, the three of us were a chain of desire.

When Dahlia resumed her attentions to Fen, he came quickly. His grunts were primal, and as he spilled down Dahlia's throat, I pushed her toward another orgasm.

Her slick warmth and the way she clenched around me, combined with Fen's peak, were intoxicating. I gripped her hips and let go of restraint. I hammered inside her, fucking past the point of being spent. I actually could go all night, and it was tempting, but we needed some rest.

We had eternity to fuck. It was one of the sexiest thoughts I'd ever had.

As I slowed to a stop, still resting inside Dahlia, Fen collapsed next to us. Something clicked inside me, like broken pieces fitting together. Like an important thing being made whole.

Was it because I was connecting with Dahlia and Fen?

No. It was more.

Did I dare hope it was NEON?

We took our time drying each other off, then lay together in bed, curled around each other, making it difficult to tell where one of us ended and the next began.

"What's that feeling?" Dahlia asked. "That... completeness?"

"You feel that?" I shouldn't be surprised. She was a third of the reason it had happened.

Fen pulled us both closer. "Even I feel it. What is it?"

Something that might flit away if I gave it a name. But it wouldn't. Things were right now, at least there. "NEON is healed." It tasted incredible to say the words.

"Yeah?" The way Dahlia's face lit up, her genuine glee, was incredible.

I sat up but kept my hands on them. "Do you want to see?"

"Yes, but also... we don't have to get dressed, do we?" Dahlia said.

"Why would we?" Fen echoed the thought in my head.

Dahlia sat and swung her legs over the side of the bed, tangling her fingers in mine. "When you put it that way... of course."

In a blink, we were in the club. It was still a mess —furniture shoved aside, walls empty—but it felt *right*. Items could be replaced, but the man and woman I loved couldn't. A heavy weight had lifted from my heart, and left joy in its place.

I'd denied that Dahlia was part of us, but I wouldn't do that anymore. The three of us were connected in a way that defied time or reason, and I wouldn't have it any other way.

CHAPTER 31

FENRIR

It took us a few days of calling in favors and hunting for just the right look for the next phase of NEON, but several immortals and supernaturals were willing to help without question. NEON had saved a lot of them in different ways, from offering a hiding place to just offering sanity in a world where they couldn't find it elsewhere. They all wanted to see it brought back to life.

Now it looked better than ever, especially given the hints of Dahlia that mingled into everything. Nothing overt, but a little more lace and a bit more purple were added to the decor. And she insisted on upgrading the entire sound system.

Frey had argued—though not with much enthusiasm—that dancers didn't need Dolby 6.2 surround sound. It wasn't as if this was a movie theater.

Dahlia made a ridiculous but valid point that it

could be. Why wouldn't we have Wednesday Movie Night?

When we'd finished remodeling, we decided it was time to invite everyone who had helped for a grand re-opening party. It wasn't the first of these that we'd had over the centuries, though *the club was destroyed* was a first.

And it would be the last time that would happen.

I stood near the doorway, watching the room. As Frey and Dahlia mingled with guests. With the vibe in here, this would become an orgy in the next few hours. Which meant Frey was back to himself. It was perfection.

Dahlia approached me. She looked the way she had when she walked in here a few months ago, looking for safety—braids, simple outfit, and mischievous grin. But under the surface, she was so much more. The same person at her core, but stronger. More confident.

I tugged one of the braids. "Handles. For me?"

"Only if you come mingle." She tugged my hand toward the group. "Introduce me to people."

"Frey can do that." I'd already seen him doing so.

She pouted and stared at me with wide baby-dragon eyes. "There's no threat here tonight."

It was true. Tonight felt safe. But, "I like to watch."

Dahlia laughed, and Frey stepped up next to her. "Am I missing the fun?" he asked.

"Fen won't mingle."

Frey wrapped an arm around her waist and nuzzled her neck. "Then let him watch." He pulled her into the crowd again, and toward a woman with a vibrant rainbow for hair. A unicorn. She'd be in a cage by the end of the night, and loving every violently sexy minute of it.

The one person who seemed out of place in the room was Magnus. She was chatting with people, mostly Brit, but it was clear she wasn't into the evening. Her smile didn't reach her eyes and she moved away from most conversations after a brief exchange.

I was worried about her. It hadn't been my dream we were caught in after Dahlia left, it was Magnus's. Now that I'd had time to reflect, I was certain of it. Her tone had changed. It wasn't that she was more willing to kill now—she'd been trained into that regardless—but she was more excited about it. The bloodlust practically rolled off her whenever vengeance came up.

A round of loud laughter drew my attention and I turned back to Dahlia and Frey, to find them surrounded by a small group. Dahlia was doing impersonations. Her dragon shifting ability let her adopt a lot of new looks. Some she couldn't quite pull off—her eyes were always hers—but she was trying.

And the entire crowd was loving her antics.

Maybe I should join them after all. See what a dragon-wolf looked like.

A movement caught my attention out of the corner of my eye, and I turned in time to see Magnus slip from the room. I needed to talk to her. The compulsion practically yanked me in her direction, so I slipped away and followed.

I found her in the back hallway, heading toward the entrance to the apartments. She stopped at the doorway that led upstairs. "You're still a shitty tail."

"I'm not trying to hide."

She faced me. "You prefer that your prey knows you're there? I kind of like that. I might ask you for a lesson or two."

There was that sensation again. Bloodlust. The potent need to destroy. I might like the feeling if it didn't clash with the lust-lust that came from the other room. "Don't fall into this pit."

"There's no pit. Or rather, not a lower one than the one I'm already in." The way Magnus smiled was terrifying. "But even if I hadn't already fallen, how well do you think telling me what to do will work?"

Not at all. I was going to try anyway. "I've been where you are. When I thought I killed Astrid..."

"Yeah, you lost yourself. Heard the story. Got the stamp in my frequent listener card. But the letting go felt good, didn't it?"

Not in a way that I would ever admit in front of

Frey. There was so much freedom in taking that leash off. "At the time, yes. Not when it was over."

"It's *not* over for me. I'm still in the middle of it." Bitterness dripped from her words, tinged with that feeling of *burn it all down*. "Don't tell me what I'll feel decades from now. I want comfort today. Besides, you had Frey."

"And you have Dahlia."

"And they tried to take her from me. Vidar did. Bragi did. You would've torn them apart if they took her from you."

I couldn't argue Magnus's point.

She scoffed. "So either help me destroy them or stand aside and let me do it alone." Her posture shifted, her expression turned more pleasant. Deceptive but neat trick. "Come on. This is violence and death. It's your wheelhouse."

I shook my head. "I'm a god of war, not vengeance."

"Because wars are always fought for just and righteous reasons, and there are never two wrong sides sending their pawns to fight their petty battles?" Her sarcasm was back.

I clenched my jaw, and tried to make myself argue her point. It was about the battle, not the reasons, but that still gave her permission. Not that she needed it.

"I did *nothing* while I was with Bragi." She spat the words with disgust. "I curled in on myself and gave up. Dahlia built a shrine to me. She called me every day. All I had to do was pick up the phone once. To not take Bragi's word for everything. Instead, I chose to stay broken and give up."

"You were healing and mourning."

"I was ready to surrender everything. Those assholes won because I stopped giving a fuck and let someone else tell me what to do. I'll take them down, and it may not make everything right again, but it will be a start." When Magnus turned a pleading look at me, I felt her desperation. "Don't try to stop me. Help me instead. Please? Not for me, but for Dahlia. All I want is a fair fight."

That wasn't true in any way. She would torture Vidar if she had the chance. Make Bragi suffer. But I didn't like the idea of helping with that. "Okay. But I won't hide this from anyone. If you want to keep it a secret from Dahlia or Frey, I'm not your guy."

"I know." Her smile was sad. "In fact, I think I'd resent you if you lied to them."

Good. Great.

A loud gasp came from a doorway next to us, and Dahlia walked into the hallway. "Oh no. My sister and my boyfriend hiding in a dark hallway. Whatever will I do?" Dahlia's hurt was exaggerated, and she pretended to faint and fall into Magnus.

"I don't know. Watch?" Magnus rolled her eyes and pushed Dahlia, so she stumbled into me instead.

I caught Dahlia and tucked her close. "I think I'm done watching for the night."

"Are we moving the party?" Frey's voice came from behind me.

"I think the orgy in the other room moved the party long before us," Dahlia teased.

Frey screwed up his face, as if focused. "Nope. There are only four of them in there. I think it takes at least five to be an orgy."

"Is that a number of holes thing?" Magnus asked. "No, wait. I don't want to know." She curtsied. "This was a beautiful party, and I'm glad you have your realm back." She sounded sincere, but sadness still lay under it all. "I'm going to bow out early, if you don't mind."

Dahlia extracted herself from me. "Are you okay?"

Magnus looked between the three of us.

"You don't have to answer that," Dahlia said.

Magnus gave a short nod. "I will be." She walked upstairs.

She needed time. Not much, but smothering her with attention wouldn't help. Time to distract my paramours. "I heard something about counting holes?"

"Pretty sure that's not how the conversation went." Dahlia was laughing again.

Frey grabbed us both. "No reason to discount a good idea, though."

For tonight, I was going to focus on the love that flowed between us. On these two incredible people. Because this feeling was potent and terrifying and incredible. An all-consuming passion of the best sort.

And I would never give it up. Never give *them* up. Because Frey and Dahlia were my forever.

CHAPTER 32
MAGNUS

I hadn't restocked my fridge since I'd been back. I tended to exist on takeout and rage. But I was hungry this morning, and in the mood to cook for myself.

Fortunately, the kitchen that sat between NEON and NEON diner was stocked again. The staff would be down there, but this early, it was likely everyone would be sleeping the party off if they were still here.

Including Dahlia and her guys.

I headed downstairs, and couldn't help pausing at NEON to take a look. There were dozens of people still here, in various states of undress and laid out on the couches and each other. Min and Kirby were still here—no surprise there. It was likely Dahlia, Fen, and Frey were in his office, or just out of view here; Queen and Kings of the evening.

Whatever. I was genuinely happy for her, but that didn't stop me from feeling a little bitter and hurt and lonely. Extra lonely. Overwhelmingly—

Stop.

I headed toward the kitchen, and the clatter grew louder the closer I got, until the clanging of silverware and shouted orders were the only thing I heard. It was nice to let that block out the voices in my head for a few minutes.

As long as I stayed out of the staff's way, and walked with purpose, no one paid attention to me. That was the trick to blending in almost any situation—look like I belonged there.

I grabbed a small, discarded box from a pile by the door, and headed to one of the fridges. From inside, I plucked a few eggs and a slab of bacon. Then I snagged a few rolls from a nearby rolling shelf full of baked goods.

As I walked toward and past the bar, to get back upstairs, my gaze drifted to the liquor. It was both a shame and a relief that I couldn't get drunk these days. Because I would if the opportunity was there, to erase the pain, because the instant I let my mental guard down, the rage and grief always roared back in. They fought until they threatened to consume me, and I was the biggest loser at the end of it all.

I stepped into the hallway and found Min talking to Dahlia. So much for avoiding people.

Min gave me a look I didn't understand. "Join us?"

I wasn't in the mood to chat, but Min was one of those gods I felt like I couldn't deny. One of those who was both ancient but still kind and humane. So I joined them.

"Dahlia told me you wore the bracer," Min said.

Fight conversation? I could do that. "It hurt like fuck, but yeah, I wore it."

"Min is familiar with the magic in the bracer," Dahlia said.

He gave a quick nod. "It is not something that gets used much anymore. The power tends to be accessible to ancient beings only. Old gods. Creatures who came before us, when they wanted to keep us young upstarts from playing with their toys."

Min had been around for a long time. Thousands of years longer than most gods, if I understood right. For him to call himself young... What was older than Min besides dragons?

Baku, apparently.

But not me. "I'm a Valkyrie. Pretty sure if Odin created the originals, that makes them *not* ancient beings."

"You're not. Mostly dragons. Baku."

No surprise there.

"Phoenixes." When Min said that, my world tilted and spun.

Did he know...? Did I dare hope? "Can you tell me about phoenixes?" Like if they lost their memory at rebirth and how to get it back.

"Nothing more than you already know." Min sounded apologetic. "Possibly not nearly as much as you know, since you have phoenix and god magic in you."

"What? No I don't." I wasn't like Dahlia. I had normal, boring parents, and was only a Valkyrie because Kirby gifted me with the honor.

"Hu—" Dahlia wobbled and planted a hand on my shoulder to steady herself, before her gaze went blank.

It was a dragon vision. They usually passed quickly, but I tended to dread what came from them.

She was muttering something, so quietly I could barely hear. I leaned closer.

"Who's a cute widdle birdie? You are. Yes you are."

What the fuck was she talking about?

After another moment of muttering and cooing, Dahlia focused on us again. On Min. "We'll let you get back to Kirby. Thank you for the information."

"Does Magnus—"

"Thank you." Dahlia talked over him, and nudged him back toward the main room.

Rude. "What was he going to say about me?" I asked.

"So you know how Min's a god of fertility? Better than a pregnancy test?" Dahlia asked.

"Yeah?" Wait. Was Dahlia pregnant?

She twisted her mouth in that way that meant she was trying to figure out the best way to phrase something. Was she having puppy-dragon babies? Was I jealous or happy for her? Happy was the right response.

"So, Nico may not be the last phoenix anymore," Dahlia said.

What? "Who's he been fucking?" My rage surged potent and instantaneously.

"You." Dahlia looked at my stomach.

All the energy drained from me and I dropped the food. The eggs cracked. I didn't care. "I'm not..." Pregnant. No. "I can't be." Gods didn't work that way.

Unless fate thought it was funny.

Dahlia looked apologetic. "I think you're pregnant. Twins. That was what the vision said."

God and phoenix magic. Bragi and Nico.

Fuck me.

THANK YOU FOR READING DAHLIA, Frey, and Fen's happily ever after.

If you're ready for the rest of Magnus, Nico, and

Bragi's story, check out EXPLOITATION and DECIMATION.

Magnus has had everything—everyone—she loved stripped from her. She has her sister back, but she'll never forgive the god who said he loved her, and she'll never forget the phoenix shifter who can't remember her.

Both men left her with a secret that will get her killed if anyone finds out.

A secret she has to tell them both, in order to survive.